So, it was her, Sandrene, his wife, not some alien replacement but deep in his heart he was still stumped.

How could she change so thoroughly? He had even had fanciful thoughts that this was Gracie instead of Sandrene, but he had heard Sandrene having a conversation with Gracie a week ago about her lovely time in St. Vincent or wherever she was.

"How is Gracie?" he asked cautiously. He didn't want to give any of his thoughts away about his fanciful suspicions.

"She is good." Sandrene looked up at him. "She is contemplating getting married to Jose."

"When is she coming home to help you out at the restaurant?" Saint raised an eyebrow.

Overwork and stress could be causing her personality change. He was grasping at straws.

THE PATIENCE OF A SAINT

BRENDA BARRETT

JAMAICA TREASURES

The Patience of a Saint

A Jamaica Treasures Book/August 2018

Published by Jamaica Treasures
Kingston, Jamaica

978-976-8247-68-1
Jamaica Treasures
P.O. Box 482
Kingston 19
Jamaica W.I.
www.fiwibooks.com

ALSO BY BRENDA BARRETT

FULL CIRCLE
NEW BEGINNINGS
THE PREACHER AND THE PROSTITUTE
AFTER THE END
THE EMPTY HAMMOCK
THE PULL OF FREEDOM
REBOUND SERIES
THREE RIVERS SERIES
NEW SONG SERIES
BANCROFT SERIES
MAGNOLIA SISTERS SERIES
SCARLETT SERIES
WILEY BROTHERS SERIES

ABOUT THE AUTHOR

Books have always been a big part of life for Jamaican born Brenda Barrett, she reports that she gets withdrawal symptoms if she does not consume at least two books per week. That is all she can manage these days, as her days are filled with writing, a natural progression from her love of reading. Currently, Brenda has several novels on the market, she writes predominantly in the historical fiction, Christian fiction, comedy and romance genres.

Apart from writing fictional books, Brenda writes for her blogs blackhair101.com; where she gives hair care tips and fiwibooks.com, where she shares about her writing life.

You can connect with Brenda online at:
Brenda-Barrett.com
Twitter.com/AuthorWriterBB
Facebook.com/AuthorBrendaBarrett

Prologue

"**Y**ou are not going to believe this." Gracie walked into the restaurant manager's office where Sandrene was putting the finishing touches on the gift basket that her mother had plopped on the desk earlier and told her to make pretty.

"I believe it." Sandrene looked up at Gracie. "It's a guy, he is cute, the cutest one you've ever seen. No movie star can compare. Gracie, you realize that you have said that several times tonight."

"It is serious this time," Gracie said dramatically. "This one looks a bit unreal. I am not sure if I am not imagining him."

Sandrene snorted. "So, what are you doing in here then? You should be out there ogling him like you do all the others."

"I am nervous." Gracie blinked twice and then slumped in the chair across from the desk. "I saw him and then immediately my limbs began to shake, and my mouth became dry. It's too much. He looked at me, and it was like a magnet drawing me to him. His eyes are green, his complexion is like caramel, and his hair brown and curly."

"He must be something to make the unflappable Gracie tremble." Sandrene chuckled and then changed the subject.

"How is the General liking his retirement party?"

"He is having fun, I guess. Mom says she doesn't want me near the main table, but it doesn't matter because the guys out there are scrumptious. They are either current soldiers or retired. All of them are fit, hard, good-looking men. Even the older ones can get a second glance. You are missing out Sands. This is the night when you should be serving, not in here pretending to study."

"I am not pretending." Sandrene pointed at her pile of books. "Does that look like pretending to you?"

Gracie shook her head in pity. "A degree in management. You know that is ridiculous, right? Mom and Dad will have you working here with or without a degree. You should do like me. Get an associate degree in something fun, like event planning, and then start working immediately. If only the parents would take my suggestions seriously and allow me to only plan parties. Instead, they have Sasha shadowing my every move."

"You graduated last week," Sandrene opened her eyes wide. "You need the experience."

"I have been working here since I was a tot!" Gracie snorted. "A tot! More faith in my abilities would be nice."

"And now you are all of nineteen." Sandrene grinned. "I am sure they will have faith in you once you get your feet wet a little."

Gracie frowned, "I doubt that. I am not their precious, responsible Sandrene."

Sandrene sighed. "Your insecurities are showing again."

"It's true though." Gracie pouted. "My parents prefer you

to me. They always have and always will."

"You know that is not true," Sandrene said patiently.

Gracie went to the mirror at the corner of the office and twisted back and forth. "It is true. How do I look?"

Sandrene answered patiently. "You look the same as you did when you came in here ten minutes ago. You look good. Fabulous."

"Why do I ask you? You have my face." Gracie headed to the en-suite bathroom and looked into the mirror, "and my body. Don't you think our butt is too flat? I should get butt pads; you know the ones that make your butt look perky and round?"

"Your butt is fine," Sandrene murmured. She had heard it all before. Gracie was as restless and insecure about her body as it was possible to be.

"I guess, it is proportional to the body but what about the breasts? I should get a push-up bra that does things to my chest. I look like a sickly waif." Gracie howled in despair. "Why couldn't my shape be more bodacious and less string bean?"

Sandrene looked down at herself. She had the same shape as her sister, but she was not shapeless.

She was convinced that Gracie had body dysmorphia, or maybe she was being typical Gracie—over the top, dramatic, and dissatisfied within herself.

"I should hike up my skirt and put on some more makeup. My eyelashes look too sparse!"

Sandrene rolled her eyes. How was it possible that they were identical in looks but so opposite in personalities?

They were exact replicas and had no distinguishing features. Not one. Staring at Gracie was like staring in a mirror.

Their parents had only managed to tell them apart when

they were babies because of their temperament.

Gracie had been a moody child, constantly crying and throwing tantrums and Sandrene had been the calm one. She didn't make waves and was easy to forget.

Gracie on the other hand, could not be ignored. She had been creating havoc since birth.

Her mother said that every gray hair was courtesy of Gracie's antics. Gracie was the one who got into fights, would fight boys twice her size and age, and was a spitfire through and through.

Though Sandrene and Gracie looked identical, shared the same parents and lived in the same household, they had very different upbringings. They hadn't even gone to the same schools when they were younger; Gracie was expelled from private prep school when they were eleven and had to be homeschooled for a year leading up to high school. After a torrid couple of years in a private high school, she had rebelled and ran away from home at fifteen to live in a Rastafarian commune in the hills of St. Andrew.

Luckily, six months in, someone from the community had seen the missing person bulletins on television and reported it to the police.

Her parents had gone for a defiant Gracie who had been renamed Empress Royal by her new tribe. She had been living with her king, Ras Simeon.

As bad as the situation was, there was one positive that came out of it. When Gracie came back, she wasn't as restless. She had been conscious and spiritual and striving to be humble.

All of that wore off by the time Gracie turned sixteen. She had eschewed all her Rastafarian views. Sandrene doubted that Ras Simeon would recognize his empress now.

A year ago, Gracie had dyed her hair blond and added

extensions that were almost hip length. She had also started wearing non-prescription colored contacts. Today her eyes were blue. Yesterday they were gray.

Sandrene wondered, how identical twins could be so different. She and Gracie were as different as night and day, opposites, that ironically looked the same.

Gracie desperately wanted to be an individual and not part of a twin. However, Sandrene had always wished she had a connection with her twin. She sometimes wished that they were good friends and not just sisters who happened to look alike and share the same DNA.

She had friends at school who were closer to her than her twin sister! She didn't dare share any confidences or secrets with her twin because it was bound to get broadcasted or ridiculed.

She hated that she had to be on constant guard around her sister.

"That's cute," Gracie said walking back into the room. "I envy that arrangement skill."

Sandrene smiled. It was a rare compliment from Gracie.

"Anyway," Gracie hiked up her skirt another inch, "I am going back to work. Wish me luck. I am going to see if I can get that green-eyed guy's name and number."

Sandrene cleared her throat. "When you hike up the skirt, the split at the back looks indecent. It goes way too far."

"Don't care." Gracie giggled. "I think this will do the trick."

"Done with the basket?" Sanya walked into the office.

"Yes," Sandrene nodded. "All done."

"Shouldn't you be at work?" Sanya raised an eyebrow at Gracie.

"I am going," Gracie grumbled, "just came to freshen up."

Sanya turned back to Sandrene. "We need extra help with the wait staff. One of the girls is down with a stomach bug.

Can you give us the extra hours?"

"I have to study, Mom." Sandrene groaned. "I have an exam tomorrow, and it is the dreaded Economics."

"I know." Sanya nodded, "but it's just for two hours, and the party is winding down. There are extra uniforms back there. I will not forget this act of kindness."

Sandrene chuckled. "You always say that."

"And I never do. Did I hear someone say that they liked my pink Gucci bag?" Sanya winked at her and then glimpsed Gracie's retreating back. "That girl is going out into the courtyard with the split in her skirt almost up to her butt. Where did I go wrong with her?"

Sanya hurried after Gracie and Sandrene went to put on a uniform.

****

Saint Wiley was sitting at a table of eight with members from his past squad, and his best friend, Maxwell.

Max was recounting one of their military training adventures when they had to hike up a mountain with a heavy pack nearly twice their size in the middle of the night.

"Saint rescued me one night. I almost fell off a cliff up there in the Blue Mountains. If he hadn't, wild pigs would have eaten me, and you would never hear about me again." Max slapped Saint on the back. "Did I tell you thanks, man? My future children thank you and my future wife thanks you."

"Every day for the last two years," Saint smirked. "And the future wife and kids are all welcome."

The rest of the table laughed, and somebody else launched into another story, but Saint was not listening.

He was watching the new waitress. The one with the short

curly hair, it was cut in the same style as his. The style suited her face. She had the cutest little ears and flawless dusky brown skin.

His eyes followed her around the room.

"She looks like the blond-haired girl that has been looking over here all night."

"Huh?" Saint dragged his eyes from the girl and back to Max.

"The one in the short skirt, blue eyes," Max murmured. "They could be twins, except for the hair and eyes."

"Never noticed her," Saint whispered. "There is something about that one that I find fascinating."

"She looks like a less colorful version of the other one." Max chuckled. "The blond was practically drooling in your direction when you walked in."

Saint grunted. "I don't care I want to meet that one."

He nodded in the other girl's direction. She was busy with other customers and had no idea she was the cynosure of his attention.

"I am sure that will be no problem at all," Max snickered. "Women inexplicably throw themselves at you. I have no idea why."

Saint grinned. "I am a nice person."

"It must be that. Your niceness shines through your pretty face." Max chuckled. "There is the other girl. If I didn't have a girlfriend, I'd be interested. It would be interesting if we dated twins."

"Maybe." Saint looked at the girl who was heading their way, and it stunned him that he hadn't noticed her before. She was a bolder, brighter version of the girl he liked.

She stopped at the table. "Everybody all right?"

Saint shook his head, and their eyes met.

"You sure?" she quirked an eyebrow at him. "If you want

anything at all I can get it."

Saint shook his head, but she still sashayed over to his side of the table with an exaggerated twist of her hips.

"Hey you," she said breathily, bracing out her chest in a come-hither manner.

"Hi," Saint smiled at her. He found her exaggerated movements funny. "What's your name?"

"Sandrea Grace Russell but most people call me Gracie." She spoke close to his ear and then pulled back looking in his eyes. "What's yours?"

He jokingly gave her his full name just like she had done. "Saint Noel Wiley."

"Saint Noel, were you born on Christmas Day or something?"

"That's right." Saint nodded.

"Are your eyes real or fake?"

"Real." He smiled.

"They are so pretty. You know I was born on Christmas Eve."

"Is that so?" Saint grinned. "Now, isn't this a coincidence?"

"It is," Gracie nodded vigorously. "I would say it is a happy coincidence we could party together this year. It would be fun."

"Me, you and your twin," Saint searched for her sister in the busy restaurant. "What's her name?"

"Sandrene Hope Russell." Gracie saw him looking at her sister a bit too long and then smiled wickedly. "You are not her type. She is into girls."

"Oh," Saint frowned. He didn't believe Gracie. The smug way she said it did not quell his interest in Sandrene.

"Such a pity," he said out loud and looked at Gracie lazily. "A real tragedy."

"I know." Gracie shook her head in exaggerated sadness."

The parents are trying to pray it out of her, God bless them, but she is who she is."

"I see," Saint murmured.

"But I am different. We are identical in everything but that. Here's my number." Gracie handed him a piece of paper with her number on it. "Call me."

Saint tucked the paper in his pocket. He wasn't going to call Gracie. He wanted Sandrene's number though.

****

"Did you see him?" Gracie gushed later in the night.

Sandrene looked up at her sister blearily and slapped her diary shut. She knew who the 'him' was. She didn't need to ask. She was writing about him in her diary. She hoped Gracie never saw what she wrote.

"Yes, I did. He is gorgeous as you said." She answered dismissively.

"And he likes me!" Gracie spun around the room and then sat on the floor. "His name is Saint Noel Wiley. We talked. He sounds so refined. You know, like one of those guys that read the news. I think he is wasted in the military. He should be on television, seriously, as a romantic lead in a movie."

Sandrene grunted. "I guess."

"You guess!" Gracie squealed. "If you are pretending that you are not into him it is not working. Anybody with eyes can see that he is out of this world gorgeous."

Sandrene had no answer for that. For the first time in her life, she was envious of Gracie. She usually couldn't stand the guys that Gracie liked. They were usually thugs with tattoos who called her sister, little woman, and shorty and who cussed after every two words. The thought of them made her shudder in distaste.

Until now there had not been any doubt that she and Gracie would ever have the same taste in men.

But there was a first time for everything.

She had been on her way to the office to get her books and to head home when Saint was on his way out with the rest of his party.

He had stopped in the lobby area to discuss something with his friend. The friend, she had noted, was as dark as he was light. They were both tall almost the same height, broad-shouldered and leanly muscular.

She didn't know if it was coincidental or not, the song Iris by the Goo Goo Dolls was playing in the restaurant. It was her favorite late nineties song, and she was singing loud enough while crossing the lobby.

'And I don't want the world to see me, Cause I don't think that they'd understand, I just want you to know who I am...'

They both turned to look at her when she walked by, but her eyes met and held with the compelling green ones.

She now understood the literal meaning of double take.

The guitar riff of the song played in what seemed to her to be a longer than usual eye contact, which she had broken off belatedly. She had her hand on the connecting door to the admin offices when she had spun back around.

He stood there looking at her. His hands were in the pockets of a black jeans. He was wearing an olive-green shirt that emphasized his green eyes.

He inclined his head and stared at her while she stared at him, unable to move.

His friend broke the spell by saying something to him, and handsome-green-eyes broke eye contact. She had fled into the office, her heart beating triple time as if she had just run a marathon.

It had been significant. It had felt like a movie moment. It felt like they had touched.

"Do not get any ideas about Saint," Gracie intruded in her reverie, "none whatsoever. He is mine. I saw him first."

"Don't be ridiculous." Sandrene snorted. "There is no guarantee that Saint likes either of us."

Gracie frowned. "He likes us all right. He couldn't keep his eyes off you when he was sitting at the table. Only time will tell which version he likes better. I am betting me. It has to be me, or I will just die. I gave him my number, and I am waiting for him to call."

Chapter One

Five years later...

"**A**re you coming to the wedding?" Saint leaned on the door to the guest bedroom where Sandrene was lounging on the bed in a state of undress. She was texting on her cell phone and didn't immediately respond.

When she deigned to lift her head, there was a frown between her eyes as if she had forgotten the question and had to recall what he asked.

"Why, is it today?"

"No." Saint tried not to snarl, but some of it transferred to his voice. "The wedding is Sunday. We are having all weekend celebrations. Mostly everyone is in Portland already. Case is driving over with us if you are coming."

"I have events at the restaurant booked all weekend." Sandrene shrugged. "Guy's wedding completely slipped my mind. It's not as if your family will miss me. They hate when

I am around. They hate me!"

Saint nodded. "I see."

"That was a loaded I see." Sandrene placed her hands on her hips and turned to him quirking one shapely eyebrow. "You think I am overreacting?"

"No," Saint shook his head. "They can't stand you, the new you. They liked you very well before you started acting like a..." Saint sighed. "I do not want to argue today. I am all out. This whole thing is draining. Besides, I am determined to be in a good mood starting today. This is a happy occasion for my family."

"So, since you are determined not to feel miserable." Sandrene winked at him, "want to do a quickie while the bed is still warm?"

"Not interested." Saint ran his fingers through his hair in frustration. "Sandrene, it has been four months...four long months of you acting like a jerk. You threatened to move out last month, and I had no issue with that. Why don't you do it before I get back from Portland? I can't do this anymore."

Sandrene gasped and placed a hand over her breast. "Oh Saint. I thought you would have some patience with me. I am trying here."

"No, you are not!" Saint growled. "You changed and not for the better. I can't take this anymore."

"You are just giving up on our marriage?" Sandrene purred, loosening her silky robe and standing before him, in all her shapely glory. "Four years of marriage, down the drain just like that?"

Saint was not moved. There was something wrong with his libido when it came to his wife.

It was the same body, more or less. She had turned into a gym fanatic, and her hourglass figure was honed to perfection. In the past, just one glimpse of her would drive him crazy, but not today.

In the past, just the hint of her taking off her clothes would be enough for him to tumble her down on the bed and he would be hard pressed to leave.

In the past, he wouldn't be looking her up and down dispassionately, unmoved. It was puzzling him.

It was the same come-hither smile on cherry red lips that needed no lipstick to enhance the bow-shaped pout. The same deep bronze skin that had its own glow from top to bottom.

They had married early. He had just been twenty-four years old and she twenty. He had genuinely thought at the time that he would love her forever. He had never been as attracted to another woman as he had been to her. It hadn't been just lust either. It had been a deep abiding certainty that she was the woman for him.

He couldn't imagine a time when he wouldn't be attracted to her. Sandrene had always had a lightning effect on his libido. Just a smile was enough to turn him on.

But now he found himself glowering in resentment.

"Put your clothes back on. I am serious. I want you gone."

She shrugged back into the sheer nightgown. "Okay, your loss. I gave you a shot at me for old times sakes. Maybe we could have made a go at this marriage, but you for some reason you are acting like a beast. I can only assume that you are cheating on me."

She sat down at the dressing table and looked at him dispassionately. "I knew this day would come. There is no way you wouldn't succumb to one of those women throwing themselves at you."

Saint groaned out loud. "Sandrene, this is just one example of how different you've been. In the five years since we have been together, you have never accused me of that. You have always known that you were enough.

"We had the kind of sex life that people only dreamed about. There has never been anybody else for either of us. And we loved it that way. We had none of the messy crap from previous relationships or jealous baggage."

Sandrene looked at him sharply. "I was your first? That's crazy. You are so handsome and so many women..."

"That's it," Saint moved away from the door, "It's either you have a personality transplant or a memory block. Were you in an accident that I don't know about, hit your head? I need to know."

Sandrene stopped brushing her cap of curls and put down the brush contemplatively. "I haven't had an accident."

Saint looked at her regretfully. "I think we need the space, don't you think? We can't go on this way."

Sandrene nodded. "Yes... er... I think we need some distance."

Then she breathed out and looked at him a glint in her eye. "I got married too young. I want to be with other people... see what it's like.

"My life up to now has been a drudge. I hate living here in your Wiley Complex. I hate the other wives. I hate your brothers. You are all like a hive mind, thinking and acting like you are all some kind of goodie two shoes.

"I hate their wives and girlfriends. I hate your church. I hate everything about this sorry life. I want out."

Sandrene gave him a defiant look. "I thought it would have been different. Sorry."

Saint didn't respond, every single hate that she just spewed felt as if they nailed him to the floor. He could remember a time when all of those hates had been loves.

Sandrene had loved living in the complex. She got along well with his brothers, she, Shawn, Sheryl, and Aisha had developed friendships. Sandrene loved the community ministries at church, especially the street feeding program. She didn't mind going out into all types of weather to help starving people. She used to be kind to strangers, to her family, even her messed up twin sister, who didn't get along with anybody for long. He used to think that Sandrene got all the good and Gracie got all the evil. Now he was rethinking that.

"Excuse me." She brushed past him and headed to the wall closet where they kept the suitcases.

That was the closest that they had come in four months. After the initial weeks of him being puzzlingly unresponsive to her. They had slept in separate rooms.

Saint looked at her as she grabbed the bags, throwing them unceremoniously into the hallway in an un-Sandrene like manner.

Something wasn't right with her. A woman didn't go from loving, attentive and sweet to a harpy who hated everything, without some underlying condition. Maybe somebody messed with her brain while she slept.

He squashed the thought. His explanations for the new Sandrene had gotten wackier by the day. He had resorted to reading science fiction to get answers. The brain switch was his latest theory. He had already considered the AI replacement theory.

Saint was swimming in a quagmire of ridiculousness, and he couldn't help it. He had done the pragmatic thing and used up all the security experts at his disposal. He had tested her DNA against the one he had on file. It came back as an exact match.

So, it was her, Sandrene, his wife, not some alien replacement but deep in his heart he was still stumped.

How could she change so thoroughly? He had even had

fanciful thoughts that this was Gracie instead of Sandrene, but he had heard Sandrene having a conversation with Gracie a week ago about her lovely time in St. Vincent or wherever she was.

"How is Gracie?" he asked cautiously. He didn't want to give any of his thoughts away about his fanciful suspicions.

"She is good." Sandrene looked up at him. "She is contemplating getting married to Jose."

"When is she coming home to help you out at the restaurant?" Saint raised an eyebrow.

Overwork and stress could be causing her personality change. He was grasping at straws.

Her parents had gone to Australia to help with their son's Jamaican restaurant franchise; Gracie was gone to St. Vincent to be with Jose. Sandrene was now solely responsible for the Waterfalls restaurant. It was a favorite restaurant with many high-end clients, and they always had an event going. Sandrene had to simultaneously plan events and see to the day to day running of the restaurant.

"In a month." Sandrene glanced at him balefully. "She said that last month. She is so over the moon happy with Jose that I have no idea if she means it. I will have to hire a manager. Mom and Dad are not in a hurry to come back either."

Saint nodded. "That would be a good idea, at least you could get help."

"But I'll be out of here as you have wanted for a long time. Have you ever thought that you are the problem?" Sandrene asked, a hint of vulnerability in her voice. "I mentioned moving out because I wanted to know what you would say, but you jumped on the idea."

And he still thought it was best. Saint didn't bother to deny it. "We need some space."

"Well, I'll be at Gracie's apartment." Sandrene huffed,

passing him with the bags and heading to the guest room.

Then she stopped at the door and glared at him. "You have my permission to see other people. Live a little, sow those wild oats you never got to sow. Take a mistress or two or ten. I don't care."

Saint leaned on the wall and laughed humorlessly. "You don't care because you'll be doing the same?"

"Oh yes," Sandrene smacked her lips. "Definitely! I need to live a little myself."

Saint shrugged. "Well, you are going to have to curtail that while we are still married to each other. I am a stickler for the marriage vows. I take my vows seriously. You vowed to forsake all others, and while you are married to me, you are going to do just that!"

"What are you going to do? Watch me around the clock?" Sandrene sneered.

"Oh yes," Saint nodded. "Twenty-four hours surveillance and you won't even know where my men are and who they are, so you cannot hide!"

"Well then, I am going to divorce you," Sandrene raged, "as soon as I can."

"Fine!" Saint snarled back. "You won't get any argument from me."

Chapter Two

"**Y**ou are driving too fast!" Case shouted at Saint, after he overtook a long line of traffic on the Long Lane Road, just before climbing Stony Hill.

Saint was forced to stop for the traffic light, and Case sighed loudly.

"I wish I had driven my car. I swear my life just flashed before my eyes."

"So dramatic," Saint murmured.

"What did Sandrene do to you?" Case asked shrewdly. "Since you slammed your way out of your house, you have been acting like a bear with a sore paw."

"She is moving out." Saint grimaced. "She wants to see other people, and she told me I should sow my wild oats like I never did in my youth. I am just having a delayed reaction to it. I can't believe I didn't blow up when she said it."

"What did you say?" Case asked.

"I said she wasn't seeing anybody else without first getting a divorce. I threatened to put twenty-four hours surveillance on her."

Case nodded. "That's right."

"And then she said, well I want a divorce then, and I said fine."

"Ah," Case looked at him concerned. "I always liked Sandrene, this is sad."

"You liked Sandrene four months ago," Saint murmured. "This Sandrene has changed beyond all recognition. She is more like Gracie."

"Maybe you should find Gracie and see if she changed into Sandrene." Case chuckled.

Saint looked at him contemplatively. "Maybe that is not a bad idea. Like a body switch Sci-Fi style."

"That sounds far-fetched," Case murmured, "but if finding Gracie will give you some insight into how Sandrene is acting, and it will save your marriage go for it."

"I am not sure anything can save this marriage," Saint grunted, "but I am not going to think about that now. It is Guy's and Lucia's weekend. They deserve all the joy and cheer from their family. Guy deserves it; he has been waiting for his woman for a long, long time."

"I agree," Case looked at him contemplatively. "Can you keep a secret?"

"Uh huh," Saint glanced at him, "have I ever disclosed any of your secrets to anyone?"

"What about the time at Georgia's house party that you told Preston on me after you found me smoking with the guys at the back."

"That doesn't count," Saint snorted. "You were twelve. You have asthma, and you were a budding singer. You deserved to be told on."

Case grunted. "I guess, but I had never seen Preston so

mad. You know he punished me severely...treated me like a prisoner for a year."

Saint chuckled. "I know, I was there. I suggested it. It was just enough time for your new smoking friends to forget you. Tell me your secret. I won't tell unless you are in danger and I need help to bail you out."

"It's not a matter of bailing me out." Case sighed. "I did something years ago when I was nineteen. It has been weighing on my mind since."

"What is it?" Saint glanced at him, "just spill it. No judgment."

"I bought a girl." Case sighed. "Yes buy, as in commodity. Buy as in human trafficking."

"What! Why?" Saint raised an eyebrow.

"We were in my dressing room after a concert in Cuba when this woman got past security and brought a dirty, emaciated child into the dressing room and said, here is Lyla, you sing about God and how good he is, God told me that she is yours, for just five hundred US dollars."

Saint slowed down significantly. "Say what?"

"I was shocked, my manager Jules was shocked. The promoter, Juan, was in there as well and he started shooing her away, but I looked at the little girl, and something impressed me to ask what will happen to her if I don't buy her?

"And the lady responded. 'I'll sell her to Santiago. He prefers girls as young as twelve, but this one is fourteen and getting a bit long in the tooth. He'll pay me just a fifty for her. I figure since you are a foreigner and a big-time singer you can afford ten times that."

Case inhaled raggedly. "What was I supposed to do? She was a skinny rag of a child with big brown eyes that pleaded with me to save her."

"And did you?" Saint asked.

"I did," Case cleared his throat, "bought her for one hundred and fifty dollars. Juan had bartered with the woman to reduce the price to one hundred dollars."

"This is not a serious story," Saint frowned, "is it?"

"It is," Case sighed. "Juan said that parents sold their young girls all the time in exchange for money and trinkets. He said that droves of men from other countries came to the country and sought out underage girls for sex. Even girls as young as eight."

"Crikey." Saint shuddered. "So, what happened to her?"

"After I bought her, I can't believe I am casually saying this about a human being. I had to marry her to get her out of the country."

Saint pulled over to the side of the road and turned to his brother. "What?"

"I married her." Case inhaled raggedly. "It was the only thing to do at the time. It is legitimate; we didn't say vows or anything like that, we just signed the papers.

" The papers were drawn up in no time, and I carried my bride back to Jamaica and gave her to Jules' mother to raise and to teach English. She hadn't spoken the language before. I haven't seen her since."

Saint shook his head. "I can't believe this!

"Believe it." Case sighed. "I provide for my 'wife' through my lawyer. Rita seems to like her, she is always sending me updates about her, but I never see her. I am too busy and not interested. Now for my current dilemma. I am engaged to Fifi. Before she went to Africa, I asked her to marry me."

"Where is Fifi? Saint asked. "I haven't seen her around in months."

"She is conquering the African continent, you know she is a hot evangelist right now. They love her over there." Case shook his head. "Fifi has a crazy schedule for the next six months. She is visiting countries like Botswana, Namibia, Malawi, Gambia, Ivory Coast, and a couple more.

"She wanted me to come with her as her singing evangelist, but I declined. I did the African tour years ago, visited nearly twenty-seven countries. That's half of the countries by the way. I think Africa has fifty-four countries."

"I know." Saint was trying to process the incredible news that his baby brother was a married man. "So, have you seen your wife lately?"

"No," Case frowned, "and I don't want to. I did a good deed, though distasteful. I may have saved her from a terrible life."

"Have you told Fifi that you are not single?" Saint asked. "Because she thinks that she is engaged to you for real."

"I have time." Case shrugged. "I am booked until next year. Fifi is booked until next year. When we take a break, which both of us could desperately use, we'll discuss our relationship. Lyla is graduating college next year. She'll probably welcome an annulment so that she can move on with her life."

"This is mind-blowing." Saint whistled. "Aren't you curious about seeing her now?"

"No." Case chuckled. "I am too busy. I love what I do, and I am happy that I could help when I could, but I didn't marry her for some romantic reason. I wanted her to have a better life. An annulment will be a gift."

"You are not even curious to know if she can now speak English fluently?" Saint persisted. "Or how she looks?"

"Nope," Case said smugly. "Rita reports that she is gorgeous, I believe her."

"You've always liked older women." Saint grinned, "how much older is Fifi than you?"

"Just twelve years." Case shrugged. "She is thirty-seven."

"Sharla hates the age gap and hates Fifi."

"I know," Case chuckled. "I was in Florida two weeks ago, she got all weepy on me and said I was marrying my mother because I grew up without one."

"Could that be remotely true?" Saint started the car and pulled into traffic.

"No." Case grinned, "I love Fifi."

"But you two hardly see each other. Saint protested. "Your relationship with Fifi is strange, and you work too hard."

"I do work hard." Case smiled. "Next year I'll slow down and then do an album."

Saint frowned at him. "You can't be doing this for the money. Your appearance fee alone is mouthwateringly high, and you are always booked. Walter decided to do a ridiculous ranking system to see which one of us who is not directly involved in the supermarket is doing the best. And you know who is making the most money this year?"

"Who?" Case chuckled.

"You." Saint shook his head. "I can never understand it. I have a flourishing top of the line security business. I employ over a hundred people. Guy has several farms, Jordan has an engineering firm, he is even turning down jobs and you just... sing. And you are topping us. What is this world coming to, when food, security, roads, and buildings are topped by singing?"

Case laughed. "I don't have the kind of overheads you and Guy and Jordan have, and my management team is aggressive. Besides, live performances and merchandise are where the money is, and I frequently do live concerts to sold out venues."

Saint snorted. "Maybe I should quit my business and manage you. They make what twenty/ thirty percent off you?"

Case laughed. "You could try, but you wouldn't like it. You have the James Bond, super spy thing going on, that's what you love. Managing me would be boring for you."

"Yeah," Saint nodded, "it would be."

"Even when we were kids you would find a mystery in anything that is not the least mysterious."

Saint chuckled. "Mystery is lurking everywhere."

"Even at your home," Case said solemnly. "You should view this whole Sandrene thing as a giant mystery and solve it before you give up on your marriage. I mean her personality change is not normal."

Saint contemplated what Case said and then nodded. "You have a point."

Chapter Three

The venue for the wedding was Micky's place at the top of the hill. The wedding was supposed to begin near sunset so that they could get the twilight glow and also the full moon rise.

According to Guy, he didn't want the traditional trappings of a wedding, just the vows between him and Lucia. There would be no wedding party with bridesmaids and groomsmen and frills. There definitely would be no reception speeches. Guy was never into public speaking.

If Walter had not taken over the planning of the wedding, it would have been just the vows at Micky's at sunset because that was the only thing that Guy had insisted on, the timing of the vows.

"Why a sunset wedding though?" He asked out loud to Case while they were on their way from the house on Spring Street. "I have never heard of a sunset wedding, well not locally. I mean tourists do it, but locals like to get married in broad daylight."

Case snickered. "Guy has his reasons. I am looking forward to it though. I have never been to a night wedding and knowing that Walter put this together, I can only imagine that it will be spectacular."

Saint nodded. "That's all he spoke about last night. You would be excused if you thought he was the one getting married. Why do we have to wear all white?"

"Because of the pictures." Case grinned, "Lucia said she wanted an all-white wedding and Walter insisted on it as if it were a law or something."

"Mmmph," Saint murmured. "I guess it will all make sense... all white wedding in the night while it's full moon."

"It should be aesthetically pleasing." Case unbuttoned his top shirt button.

Saint glanced at him. "I thought you looked a little like a trussed-up chicken, that's better."

Case grinned. "I want to be like you when I grow up—all urbane and sophisticated."

"Oh, shut it." Saint grinned. "It just goes without saying, no tie, no need for the top to be buttoned all the way up."

Case massaged his neck. "I had a rough night last night. I can't believe we used to sleep on those beds. Why did Shawn convince me to let out my villa as an Air B and B? I would have been comfortable last night. I would have slept like a king at my palace."

Saint chuckled. "She convinced me too. My place is booked all summer. I slept fine, but then again I am used to sleeping anywhere on the floor, standing up with a gun in hand."

"Show off," Case muttered, "absolute show off."

"Military training will do that to you." Saint grinned, "when I train my men now, and they complain I have a good laugh.

The Jamaica Defense Force has some of the most rigorous training in the world. You know, I prefer hiring people who went through the JDF training and earned a certificate of completion."

Case looked at him admiringly. "You did some tough stuff, didn't you?"

"Real tough," Saint snorted. "I remember when I came home after Phase two of the training, Jordan looked at me in pity and said, you can't go back. You have to quit. They are trying to kill you."

Case laughed. "Why did you do it?"

"I did it for the training. It was a part of the grand plan. I always knew I would be in the security industry. So, I got my black belt in karate and my degree in cybersecurity. I don't like wasting time. If I want something, I go after it."

"Not even with Sandrene," Case mused, "you met her one day and came home and told us that she was the woman you are going to marry."

"That's right." Saint smiled ruefully, "I was never more certain about anything."

"You should capture that feeling and hold it and never forget it." Case looked at him meaningfully, "especially now."

****

When Saint drove up the hill to Micky's, he was not sure what he would find, but it was not a winter wonderland. The place was transformed into an unrecognizable oasis of whites and twinkling lights. Walter had outdone himself this time. It was spectacular.

The white clothing made sense when he saw the setting. Most persons were dressed appropriately.

The wedding arch was under a flowering jasmine tree, which explained the strong perfumy scent in the air. Guy was already standing at the arch and chatting with Pastor Tate.

There were two rows of seats in white. Most persons were seated already. His brothers were sitting in the front with their families. Saint made his way to the front and sat between Jordan and Preston.

Jordan leaned over to him and whispered. "Guy thought that this would be a simple wedding."

Preston chuckled. "He had no idea what he was in for when he told Walter to do what he wanted."

Saint smiled. "I should have had Walter do my wedding. He is truly a creative thinker. This is spectacular."

"I know," Preston mused, "instead you had Gracie do it."

"Maybe that's why my marriage is a bust," Saint said humorlessly.

"Think happy thoughts." Jordan elbowed him. "This is a happy occasion."

Saint nodded. "Yes, thank you for the reminder. I don't want to be the lone wet blanket around."

"That's the spirit." Jordan nodded. "Tomorrow at dinner we can have a brotherly pow-wow about this."

Saint made a face. I don't want to have a brotherly pow wow. I am tired of it. I am over it."

Jordan looked at him with disbelief stamped on his face. "Somehow I doubt that. You once told me that you would rather die than give up Sandrene."

"And he said he found perfect when he found Sandrene," Preston whispered. "This is just a phase. Remember those passionate declarations before you give up on your perfect woman."

Saint was spared from answering when the saxophonist

started playing, If I were a Carpenter, as the bride glided down the aisle in a white off the shoulder dress and a crown of white flowers in her curly hair.

They looked good together, Saint thought. Like they were made for each other.

And then they were saying their vows.

Guy was the first to speak. "Lucia, on this special evening, I give to you in the presence of God and all these witnesses my promise to stay by your side, in sickness, and in health, in joy and in sorrow, through good times and bad.

I promise to love you without reservation, comfort you in times of distress, encourage you to achieve all of your goals, laugh with you and cry with you, grow with you in mind and spirit, always be open and honest with you, and cherish you for as long as we both shall live."

And then it was Lucia's turn:

"Guy, I join my life with yours. Wherever you go, I will go; whatever you face, I will face. For good or ill, in happiness or sadness, come riches or poverty, I take you as my husband, and will give myself to no other."

Tears came to Saint's eyes, and he blinked them away rapidly. These were the kind of emotionally charged vows he had shared with Sandrene.

She had said, I take you as my husband, and I will give myself to no other, and he had said that he would cherish her for as long as they both lived.

They had both failed to keep their promises.

He couldn't help casting his mind back to the early years, when he couldn't get her out of his mind.

The months of turning into a stalker as he had developed a fascination with her that had bordered on obsession.

He had loved Sandrene with every bit of fervor as she had loved him, what on earth had gone wrong?

Chapter Four

Mid-Summer, Five Years Before

"**H**ere is her file, boss." Garland slapped down a file on his desk and then sat across from him. It had been two weeks since General Cross' retirement dinner. He eagerly picked up the file with the name Sandrene Russell scrawled across the top.

Garland had pictures in it. Many pictures. He studied each of them while Garland patiently watched him and waited for his next assignment. Garland had already told him that trailing Sandrene was like watching paint dry.

"The girl is boring, boss."

He didn't care. He swiveled in his new chair. They had just furnished and painted the top floor of the Wiley Securities Building. They had started on the first floor and had gradually moved up floor by floor as they got one major contract after another and expanded the services they offered.

The private investigation division was understaffed and oversubscribed. He needed Garland elsewhere, not trailing a nineteen-year-old girl who was void of intrigue.

She went to school, pursuing a bachelors degree in the culinary arts. She sang on the church choir and had study groups with a mixed crowd. She worked from three to ten as a waitress at her parents' restaurant and sometimes as a pastry chef. She made the sweet treats on Wednesdays and Thursdays. He had tasted her baked Alaska, the baklava and the chocolate soufflé. They were all good but what did he know, he was not a food connoisseur.

He glanced at her picture again. Garland had a future career as a photographer; though it was not necessary for investigative work, he used the rule of thirds technique quite nicely on all the pictures of Sandrene. She was a pretty girl, no doubt about it.

He studied her picture. He wasn't sure what his fascination with her was about, but it had turned him into a love-struck fool who was barely concentrating on his business. He had seen pretty girls before, spoken to them, gotten their numbers, been pursued by them, but it had not made much of a difference to him until now.

His ex-girlfriend Annika was gorgeous. She was a model who had graced many magazine covers and starred in several male fantasies.

Everybody had said how well suited they were. What a perfect couple they made. In the two years since he and Annika dated they had never really struck sparks off each other. It had not broken his heart when Annika had broken up with him via text message before he went on army training.

Nor had it fazed him when he heard that she had quit modeling and married an Italian vintner.

He caressed the photo with Sandrene subconsciously.

"The first time always makes a fool of us," Garland said gruffly.

Saint dragged his eyes from the picture. "What are you talking about?"

"The first time we realize that there is one woman in the world that can tie us up in knots without even trying."

Saint regarded the older man thoughtfully. "I am not tied up in knots."

Garland snickered. "Oh yes you are, boss. And I tell you what; I think you need to make a move. Other people are interested in her."

Saint nodded. "I think you are right. Where will she be tonight?"

"Tonight is Wednesday night. She is going to be making lava cakes. There is an advertisement about it at the restaurant. I wish this were a night when you wanted me there, but I think my investigative work is done."

Saint nodded. "I'll visit the Waterfall tonight and have some lava cake. Wish me luck."

"You won't need it." Garland chuckled. "As I said, there is no evidence that she is gay as her sister said and you are too genetically blessed to be so unsure about you being well received by Sandrene."

"Thanks, Garland." Saint nodded.

"No problem, boss." Garland shrugged. "I have a stack of other cases to get through. When are you going to hire me some help?"

Saint grimaced. "Matthew shortlisted five potential candidates that can hit the ground running. You should have help in no time. Can you check with him before you leave?"

"Sure." Garland nodded at him and left.

Saint couldn't wait for the night to come.

****

"He is here again," Gracie walked over to Sandrene and growled. "And he is asking for you."

"Who?" Sandrene asked. She was distracted with making the last batch of lava cakes; she had challenged the customers to order any version of lava cake that they desired.

So far nobody had really challenged her. Chocolate was the clear winner tonight. Everybody wanted some variation of the molten chocolate cakes. The only 'out there' request she had gotten so far was sweet potato and butterscotch.

"You know who." Gracie hissed as Sandrene shook powdered sugar over the red velvet and strawberry lava cakes for a couple who were celebrating their fiftieth wedding anniversary.

Fifty years was quite an accomplishment. Her parents were going to celebrate thirty-two years soon. Her grandparents on both sides had been married for a significant number of years as well. She loved when love lasted.

"Do you know this couple, Mia and David Little, met when they were thirteen, married when they were eighteen and are still in love? After knowing each other for fifty-five years! That is amazing. I am carrying the cakes to them personally. They deserve it."

She took off her apron and sang at Gracie. "A long and lasting love, not many people find it, but those who do their whole life through, put their heart and soul behind it..."

"Seriously," Gracie growled. "You don't want to know who wants to see you?"

"Is he going to be my long and lasting love?" Sandrene asked cheekily. "I'll soon be back, Gracie. Stick a pin in it. I want to celebrate fifty years with the Little's."

The couple grinned when they saw her. Sandrene presented their dessert with a flourish. "May you be together for fifty more years."

"Thank you, Sandy." Mia winked. "And may you find a guy to love and cherish as I have with David."

"I wish," Sandrene chuckled. "What is the secret?"

"We have never wanted to break up at the same time." Mia chuckled. "One of us has to want to fight for the relationship even when the other doesn't."

David nodded. "I second that. And a healthy dose of romance. Never ever let it die. We have eight children, went bankrupt twice, had four major surgeries between us but the romance we kept alive. Give love and show love."

"And he doesn't only mean flowers and chocolate." Mia piped in. "He gets me, and I get him. We know how the other receives and appreciates love. We do what makes the other happy."

Sandrene beamed at them. "You should take this on tour. I just learned a lot."

"Can't go on tour, too busy with the grandkids." David chuckled.

"Enjoy." Sandrene walked away contemplatively. The conversation didn't prevent her from feeling eyes on her though. She turned around and there he was.

Saint Wiley.

It was like the last time when she had seen him in the lobby, except this time she wasn't going to do a double take. She was going to scurry into the kitchen as fast as her legs would take her and then try to assess why he had this kind of effect on her.

The man didn't have to speak, and yet her hands were shaking.

She almost collided with Gracie when she entered the kitchen.

"What took you so long?" Gracie grumbled, "Chef Brown has been giving me the evil eye."

"Because I don't like idlers in my kitchen." Chef Brown growled. "And you are not contributing anything but just standing around."

"I can contribute. I can do the same thing that Sandrene does." Gracie growled. "I went to pastry school."

"Ha!" Chef Brown laughed. "Pastry school my foot, not with those nails."

Gracie made a face after him and turned to Sandrene. "So, did you talk to him or do I still have to relay the message?"

"I didn't talk to him." Sandrene swallowed nervously. "What did he say?"

"He said I should tell Chef Sandy to prepare two lava cakes. Two of her favorites, and then join him."

Sandrene gasped. "What?"

"He also said he knows you get off at ten. So, no excuses."

Sandrene grinned. "Well, okay then."

"This is not fair!" Gracie shook her head, "Why you? Technically we look the same. Why is he pursuing you? I told him you were a lesbian and he is still out there waiting for you!"

"Say what?" Sandrene frowned. "Gracie, how could you?"

"Everything comes so easy for you," Gracie said bitterly. "You are the golden child, the one who gets the good grades and the cute men. The one who everybody likes more than me. I don't get it!"

"Oh Gracie," Sandrene looked at the tears pooling at the side of Gracie's eyes. "That's not true."

"Oh yes, it is," Gracie swiped her eye. "Even our parents prefer you. First, there is Sanjay the son that can do no wrong, and then there is Sandrene, the responsible daughter the sweet daughter, the one they trust with money and their restaurant kitchen, and then there is me, Sandrea Grace the pariah. Everybody looks over their shoulder when it comes to me, double checking everything, treating me like a..."

"Get out of my kitchen with your teenage tantrums, Sandrea Grace!" Chef Brown yelled when Gracie started to get fully into her pity fest.

Sandrene sighed, this was not the first time that Gracie was repeating the same old spiel. It usually came when she was not getting her way, and it ended with Sandrene feeling sorry for her and stepping back.

She was not going to do it over Saint though. She liked him. She hadn't stopped thinking about him for the past two weeks. This was an occasion that her sister's temper tantrums and unhealthy response were not going to hold sway.

"I am going," Gracie sniffed and wiped her eye. "Should I tell him that you don't want to see him?"

"No," Sandrene said firmly. "I will be doing two lava cakes for us. I'll tell him myself."

Gracie looked at her stonily. "You suck as a sister. You suck even worse as my twin."

Sandrene shrugged. "I am used to you saying that, especially when you don't get your way."

Gracie stomped out of the kitchen.

Chef Brown chuckled. "I cannot imagine how you do it, having the twin sister from hell."

"She is not usually this bad," Sandrene sighed. "Up until now, we have never liked the same guy."

"Watch out for her," Chef Brown said, "something tells me, Gracie is not going to let this go."

Sandrene nodded. "I know."

Chapter Five

Sandrene and Saint had the restaurant to themselves. The staff had already cleaned up. The main lights were off except for the candles on their table and the backlight on the bar.

It felt as if they were the only two people in the world.

They had been talking nonstop for the past hour. Saint had consumed her triple chocolate lava cake and was toying with a cup of tea which had long gone cold.

He couldn't get enough of Sandrene. He knew a good deal about her because of the investigation, but he liked to hear her talk and see her expressions. He didn't want to leave.

Sandrene leaned on the table and grinned. "You are good."

"At what?" Saint asked softly.

"You had me go on and on about myself for two hours." She looked at the clock. "You realize that it's near midnight. I want to know more about you, not yammer on and on about my life."

Saint chuckled. "Then we'll have to meet up again."

"Or talk on the phone," Sandrene said regretfully. "I have a packed day tomorrow."

"Or we can do this again tomorrow night. I'll wait until your shift ends so we can talk some more. I want to see you again. I am dreading leaving you now."

Sandrene looked at him; disbelief stamped on her face. "This is a dream, isn't it? None of this is real."

"Why would you say that?" Saint smiled and asked though he understood what she was saying. They had hit it off as if they had known each other for years.

"Because these kinds of things don't happen outside of dreams and romance novels. Gorgeous single men don't pursue ordinary women and then have intimate conversations in a restaurant courtyard after hours. I didn't even think gorgeous single men exist outside of movies and fantasies."

Saint chuckled. "There is nothing ordinary about you, and even gorgeous men have to be single sometime."

Sandrene watched as Saint talked. A little bit of disbelief still had her in its clutches. When she had approached him earlier, she was prepared for him to laugh and ask her where Gracie was.

She had peeped on him before coming out. The inside dining area had been a good cover as she watched him. All the diners had left. He was sitting alone and dressed in full black. His black turtleneck shirt emphasized his muscular arms and caramel complexion. His brown curly hair was cut in the same style as hers.

They had chatted for a while; it was amazing how much information one could learn about a person in a few minutes. She had jumped up when the timer went off for the lava cakes.

"I'll be right back." She smiled at him. "Don't go anywhere."

"I have no intentions to. I want to try that lava cake." He

had flashed his even white teeth at her.

"He is prettier than you," Her mother said when she was taking out the perfectly baked cakes. "Much, much prettier than you. That's not good."

"I know," Sandrene moaned. "But I don't care."

"He has eyes the color of my spirulina mint smoothie." Sanya grinned. "I love to see a black man with green eyes. I once dated a black guy with green eyes, very handsome, but vain, goodness!"

Sanya said wistfully. "I could deal with the vanity, but his mother was something else. She thought her son walked on water and treated him accordingly. It was too painful to deal with the mother. How is this guy's mother?"

"Dead," Sandrene said, "his parents are both dead. He grew up with his brothers. There are six of them."

"Really?" Sanya widened her eyes. "He should be clumsy around women then."

"Not at all." Sandrene chuckled. "He is great. After talking to him for a while, you'll forget that he is so beautiful and just listen to what he has to say. He is bright. It's kind of intimidating. He just started his own business, and he is thinking of going back to school to do his Masters or to do additional training in his area."

"And what area is that?" Sanya asked doubtfully. "This guy sounds too good to be true."

"Security." Sandrene giggled. "He has a security firm called Wiley Securities."

"Any relation to the Wiley Supermarket, Wiley's? Yevette snapped her fingers. "Of course, goes without saying. He looks a bit like Preston Wiley. I know Preston Wiley. He is a serious young man, very passionate about giving back and serving his community. We are on the same charity board."

"Feed the Poor Charity? Sandrene nodded. "I want to join

that."

"You should." Sanya looked at her proudly. "But back to this Saint person. You have a solid head on your body, but sometimes girls get carried away by a guy's looks. When I met your father, I concluded that looks don't mean a thing in solid relationships. So, don't get bowled over by this guy. Make sure that he loves God."

Sandrene looked at her mother and giggled. "What should I say? Hey there Saint, do you love God?"

"Yep," Sanya nodded. "Get it out of the way before you fall under his spell. If he says he doesn't, don't entertain him, no matter how gorgeous he is. You'll regret it.

Sandrene nodded. "Okay then."

"In the meantime, you know we trust you. You haven't given us a reason not to. Remember to rearm the building when you leave and don't do anything stupid. The security cameras are on."

"I am meeting him for the first time." Sandrene muttered, "What would I do?"

"Don't know," Sanya kissed her on the forehead. "But remember God and all his angels and Hemlock Security is watching. And your father checks the security feeds in the morning."

Sandrene had shakily carried out and placed the death by chocolate lava cake in front of him and smiled brightly.

"I pinned you as a chocolate lover."

He had trained his green eyes on her and then smiled slowly. "I like everything you bake. I love the Chef Sandy nights."

And she was hooked.

She had forgotten to ask him if he loved God. It seemed like such an inane question. Besides she had been caught up in the moment.

It was later on that night as they were leaving that she had asked. "Do you love God?"

"Yes," Saint had grinned, "and Jesus and the Holy Spirit. What about you?"

"Yes," she nodded.

"Well, then it's nice to get that out of the way," Saint grinned, "because if you didn't love God, it would be a problem. My name is not Saint for nothing."

Sandrene started laughing uncontrollably. "I guess not."

****

They had many more after-hours dates in the restaurant in the following months. Wednesday and Thursday nights were their favorite date nights. Sandrene made him delectable desserts and then waited for his unbiased verdict after tasting them. He liked them all.

"You should meet my brothers," Saint said after a while, "before the Christmas holidays. I told them about you. Well, I told them about you after I first saw you in the lobby. I went home told them I found her, their future sister-in-law."

"You didn't." Sandrene groaned.

"I did." Saint nodded. "And they are all dying to meet you."

"The pressure." Sandrene moaned, "it's going to be so intimidating."

"No, it won't." Saint looked at her. "Trust me. It was more pressure to meet your family."

"No, it wasn't. You are always here, and we practically live here." Sandrene grinned. "They see you all the time."

"Is that a hint that we need to go someplace else?" Saint asked, "because this is a good place to be. You are heavily chaperoned by the security cameras. Your parents can have peace of mind that I am not taking advantage of their lovely

Sandrene."

"Are we ever going to kiss?" Sandrene asked wistfully. "We have never kissed."

"Come closer," Saint whispered. "They were lounging in one of the sofas at the far end of the courtyard. They were cozily tucked between two potted trees."

Sandrene scooted closer to Saint.

"If we kiss, we might never stop," Saint whispered in her ear.

His breath made her body tingle all over.

"You may be right," Sandrene whispered back. "But who cares?"

"I care." Saint looked at her and smiled. "I think we should wait until our wedding night. You and I for the first time."

"Are you saying...?" Sandrene widened her eyes and looked at him, "but you are..."

"What, a man?" Saint grinned. "Told you I lived up to my name."

"So, when are we going to get married?" Sandrene asked seriously.

"What about tomorrow?" Saint asked huskily. "We could go to the registrar department, say the vows and then be honeymooning an hour later."

"Sounds good but I have exams, tomorrow," Sandrene said, regretfully. "I have to do them. I want to get that degree."

"And this is your final year, right?" Saint asked.

"Yes," Sandrene nodded. "One more semester to go and then I'll be free in May."

It started to rain. They could hear the spatters on the glass roof, and the lightning occasionally illuminated the place.

"And then what's next?" Saint asked lazily.

"Then I work here full time. Run this restaurant; take the load off, my parents. They are talking about opening another

Waterfalls in Montego Bay, recreating the success here, but I doubt they'll do it."

"Why?" Saint glanced at her. "What about your brother, Sanjay. I thought he was the reason for the expansion talks."

"Yes," Sandrene nodded, "but he is planning to move to Australia to be with his wife. "That's why I'll have to step in and take on more of a management role."

Saint looked around at the beautifully decorated courtyard area. It gave the illusion of them being in a garden, except there was a roof above.

"What about Gracie?"

"Gracie is more interested in event planning. She loves putting together parties. It's her thing. We could run this place together. Gracie is charming and charismatic and loves to be around people, and I am a foodie. We would make a great team."

"She growls and snarls when she sees me," Saint said wistfully. "It's disconcerting seeing her do it because she has the face of the woman I love."

Sandrene chuckled. "She resents the fact that you chose me over her. She thinks I am the ugly twin and you should have more taste."

"How can you be the ugly twin," Saint chuckled, "she looks just like you!"

"I wish we were closer," Sandrene said wistfully. "Maybe I could let her plan the wedding. She thinks that nobody trusts her to do anything. Maybe that will make us closer."

Saint smiled. "So, no courthouse wedding then?"

Sandrene frowned. "Maybe we could do it in secret and not tell anybody."

"Are you serious about this?" Saint asked, "because I am all for it."

Sandrene nodded uncertainly. "What's the sense in

waiting?"

"Well, we could get to know each other better," Saint whispered. "It has only been five months, and you haven't met my family yet..."

"I know, and I was the one who suggested that it's too early, but I want to be with you." Sandrene pulled away from Saint's arms, "I want to wake up with you in the mornings."

"I want that too." Saint cupped her cheek. "So, we need a plan."

"We elope," Sandrene said enthusiastically. "And since we are not telling our family, we'll need two discrete witnesses."

Saint nodded. "I can ask my best friend Max and my right-hand man, Matthew. They won't say anything to anyone."

"We tell nobody in our family," Sandrene said excitedly. "We'll only announce that we are engaged. They can get to plan a wedding and all of that and be happy. Gracie can even get to do her elaborate best for the wedding."

"When?" Saint asked seriously.

"When for our private wedding or the other one?" Sandrene asked.

"The private one will be at the end of this week," Saint said with certainty. "The other one."

"Next year May, after exams." Sandrene rubbed her hand in glee. "We get to have two honeymoons."

Saint pulled her closer. "I can't wait, we'll discover each other together. Do you know how rare that is?"

Sandrene looked at him her brown eyes soft with love. "Are you sure about this? Marriage is a big deal."

"I'll never love anybody but you, I want nobody but you. I am completely sure of that. Saint pulled her to him and kissed her."

****

They set the first wedding date for December 12. It was a

Friday afternoon. It was two weeks before their birthdays, and they had their ceremony at the white sand beach at Saint's cottage in Portland.

They scrapped plans to do it at the courthouse. Instead, they paid a marriage officer to do it. Max and Matthew were the two witnesses.

The bride wore a white floaty summer dress, and the groom wore white chinos and a white unbuttoned shirt. They were both barefoot in the sand.

Moments after they said their I do's, and their guests left, they found the nearest bed.

It rained all weekend, and neither of them thought to get out of bed except for food. They were inseparable after that, barely able to keep their secret from their respective families. A pregnancy scare in February almost had them changing their minds, but it turned out to be a false alarm.

Chapter Six

Saint stood at the bar and frowned at his drink. Guy's reception was in full swing. Saint had made an effort, but he was not in the party mood.

"You exhibit signs of depression," Ace Jackson said to him. "I have been watching you and waiting for an opportunity to come over and talk."

Saint looked at Ace, and he could barely drum up a smile.

"I am not in the party mood."

"Neither am I," Ace sighed. "I only came because Lucia insisted. And I didn't want it to seem as if I was a sore loser. I was this close to winning her from Guy."

Saint chuckled. "No, you weren't."

"No, I guess not." Ace sighed. "It is going to take a while for me to get over this. I had emotions invested in Lucia."

"It's life." Saint glanced at Ace. "Sometimes you win some, and you lose some. Not every story ends with a happily ever after. There are those curve balls, like divorce and separation, that complicate matters and mess with the love story."

"Yes, I know." Ace nodded. "I take it you are going through something like that."

"Yep," Saint nodded. "You are a doctor, right?"

"Last I checked." Ace chuckled.

"How can a woman who was once the sweetest, loving, attentive, considerate person turn into a selfish harpy overnight?"

"Sudden personality changes can be caused by mental illness, substance abuse, and physical illnesses such as brain infections or injury. When did you start noticing changes?"

"Around four months ago." Saint shrugged.

"You should take her to a doctor and let him explore some of these issues. He can run tests, do scans, check for drugs, check for mental erosion."

"She's twenty-four," Saint murmured. "Twenty-five this year. I don't think mental erosion is a problem.

"Besides, how on earth am I going to get her to a doctor? She seems fine, and I doubt she would listen to me anymore. She is moving out today. She is eager to see other men and have affairs. She is encouraging me to see other women as well," Saint couldn't help the bitterness that crept into his voice. "We are over."

"I know a good marriage counselor," Ace said wryly. "She must be good. My parents used her, and they are still together."

"You asked your mother about Micky yet?" Saint asked shrewdly.

"No," Ace sighed. "She is not having that conversation with me. I can't force her to speak about it. My father is worse. He has a hurt look when I ask him about my birth and as for Micky, he claims not to know anything. He tells me that I should ask my mother about it. He says she is the only one who knows the truth. I have a feeling he thinks I am his son though."

"Do a DNA test," Saint said, test them all. "Test yourself and your brothers as well. Life is too short for you to have doubts as to who your biological parents are, especially since all the players are still alive."

Ace nodded. "I'll take your advice. I'll also be calling you if I have any investigation needs. I heard your company is the best."

"We are." Saint handed him a business card. "It's a good thing I carry these around. Call me any time."

Ace moved on, and Saint made his way to the car. Everybody was having a whale of a time. He would not be missed.

He turned on the radio and drove home slowly. A wave of sadness mixed with loneliness hit him out of nowhere. It was strong enough that he had to pull over and brace himself for the impact.

It was too easy to forget the details of a relationship that worked so well when it felt hopeless.

He inhaled deeply and closed his eyes. He saw Sandrene smiling in his mind's eye, and he felt a longing for her so intense that he whipped out his phone and called Case.

"Hey, Case. I am heading for Kingston."

Case didn't hear him clearly at first, so he left the sounds of the party and went somewhere quieter.

"Are you okay?" Case asked.

"Fine." Saint sighed. "I feel strongly that I should go home."

"To sort things out with Sandrene?" Case asked.

"Hopefully. I don't know if we can be sorted. I feel a need to see her though. I hated where we left off."

"That's a good idea, don't worry about me, I will get a lift back with Preston. Apparently, they are allowing Pete to drive back, his first long-distance journey. I'll be there for the entertainment."

Saint hung up the phone and turned the music higher. It was Gerry Rafferty's Right Down the Line. His eyes teared up from the nostalgia. He sang along with the first verse, happy that he was alone. His singing voice was just okay and not up to Case's standards.

You know I need your love, you've got that hold over me, Long as I've got your love, you know that I'll never leave, When I wanted you to share my life, I had no doubt in my mind, And it's been you, woman, Right down the line...

He finished listening to the song and resolved in his mind that he wasn't going to give up his relationship. It had always been Sandrene, right down the line.

****

Saint drove up to Gracie's apartment apprehensively. Gracie's place was in a relatively large complex. She was on Block A on the third floor. He recognized the security guard at the front who waved him in without calling ahead.

Saint frowned at that faux pas. The security was not as tight as it should be and that concerned him. He would say something to the security guard when he was leaving. Sandrene may have morphed into a stranger, but she was still his wife.

He stopped at Block A and looked at the nondescript building painted in a bland shade of beige. There were three floors. Gracie had gotten an apartment on the third floor-- bought by her parents six months ago, after they had asked her to leave their house.

It had needed some repairs though, and Gracie had moved

in with him and Sandrene.

Saint frowned. That was the beginning of the end for him and Sandrene. Her insistent need to reach out to Gracie had created a wedge in their relationship and turned her into a mini Gracie in the process.

He looked around the parking lot. There was a space designated for each apartment, Sandrene's car was in the space for apartment 3A.

So, she really had moved out.

Saint didn't know what to think. He felt a pang of remorse which propelled him out of the car and up the three flight of stairs to the corner apartment where Gracie's apartment was. He had only been there once when Gracie had thrown a housewarming party after the renovations were complete and Sandrene had insisted that he come.

He had spent most of the evening on Gracie's small patio looking at other buildings. He had eventually struck up a conversation with a fellow that Gracie had been dating.

He had been a lawyer. He couldn't remember his name now, as, with all of Gracie's relationships, they were fleeting. Their names had a tendency to meld in his brain, so he remembered them by their professions. That particular guy had seemed to love her genuinely. He understood her and loved her anyway.

He was refreshingly different from the rest of Gracie's friends. He had gone on and on about Gracie and how lovely she was.

His name was Jason. Jason Garvey. He was a bit older than Gracie and had been offered a judgeship.

Saint wondered where he was now. Gracie had discarded him as easily as she did the others. After that, she went out with a janitor and then a businessman. One thing you couldn't accuse Gracie of was having a type.

Just then his mind shifted from Gracie's love life and to specific key details. The lights in the apartment were on, and he could hear soca music.

Sandrene was not a soca music fan; he had often teased her that she loved British music and Coldplay in particular than anything else.

She would play Coldplay on repeat until it drove him crazy, especially the song Green Eyes.

He pressed the door buzzer, and then he heard giggles, and the door was flung open.

He took a step back. She was dressed in a black negligee and had on a waist length blonde wig.

He shook his head and blinked. This was not Sandrene.

"Gracie! I didn't know you were home. Is Sandrene here, can I speak to her please?"

"I am not Gracie silly."

He watched the lips form the words, but he didn't believe it. There was no way this was Sandrene.

Sandrene loved her short curly hair. She didn't like it long, nor did she like wigs or weaves. She once quipped that if she lost her hair, she wouldn't mind going cleanly shaven because her head was shaped for it. He had agreed.

Added to that, Sandrene wore t-shirts and boy shorts to bed or nothing at all. She didn't own any fancy negligees like the black slinky number Gracie had on now.

"Where is my wife?" Saint asked forcefully.

Gracie widened her eyes in understanding. She couldn't pull off acting like Sandrene with Saint looking at her with contempt. "She is…she left to go on a date."

"A date?" Saint tightened his fists. "You are lying. She is in there, isn't she? Her car is in the parking lot."

"No, you can't come inside. I have company!" Gracie hissed.

Saint narrowed his eyes at her. "What aren't you telling me, Gracie? Something is not right. Is Sandrene in there?"

"No, really she is not here. She took my car. Maybe she went to the parent's house."

"With a date? In your car?" Saint ran his fingers through his hair. He felt unsettled, uncomfortable, disrupted. This whole scenario felt wrong.

"Who is this date?"

"I don't know," Gracie said. She couldn't look him in the eye when she said it, and that irritated Saint. Something was off, and he needed to get to the bottom of it.

"Well, tonight is her last date with anyone," Saint growled. "Have you noticed anything different about her?"

"No," Gracie shook her head, "not really. But I have only been back for a day. She is certainly nicer than she was before."

Saint frowned. "Nicer! Really?"

"Yep." Gracie nodded, "Way nicer, it's like since she decided to be free of you she has also gotten prettier too."

"Now, I know you are jerking my chain," Saint muttered. "How long are you staying this time? You left her to take up the slack, didn't you?"

"I know, but it can't be helped." Gracie winked at him. "Love comes first, and my honey wants us to do a cruise. We leave tomorrow, at the crack of dawn."

"I'll be gone for a couple more weeks after this."

"Can't you stay and help Sandrene? She needs the help."

"She is superhuman, the girl with everything who can do anything," Gracie said through clenched teeth. "Too bad that she couldn't keep her marriage together. Really sorry about that."

Gracie said not a lick of remorse in her voice, "but that is what you get for choosing the wrong twin. I would never throw away our relationship like this, Saint if you had married me."

Saint sighed. "Gracie, you and I never had chemistry."

Gracie snorted. "I don't get it. What's the difference? Sandrene and I are identical twins! We have the same chemistry."

"Tell Sandrene I was here." Saint turned away and then turned back. "And tell her that as of now I am watching her. My men are the best in the business."

Gracie widened her eyes. "Why are you watching my sister, it's ludicrous. She doesn't want to be with you anymore. Let her go."

"Never," Saint said, "not without a fight. Today I went to my brother's wedding, and I realized that I am not ready to give up on us. So, she had better get used to me breathing down her neck."

"She said she wants a divorce."

"She will get her divorce," Saint said, "when we have exhausted all the avenues available to us reconciling. Until then, it's on."

He missed the look of horror on Gracie's face as he walked away.

Chapter Seven

Gracie closed her apartment door and leaned on it. She wasn't a bad person. On the contrary, she was helping Sandrene out. She was running the restaurant, her sister's marriage, and everything else. With Sandrene out of the picture, she had no choice.

Of course, she would not think about the glaring fact that she was the one who had taken Sandrene out of the picture.

Her hands trembled as she moved from the door and into her bedroom.

"You will have to go," she said to the man lounging in the bed. "My brother-in-law is going to start surveilling me."

"Why?" he asked suspiciously. "What have you done?"

"None of your business," Gracie growled, "and I won't be seeing you for the foreseeable future. I'll be taking a trip, and my sister will be living here for a while."

"Where are you going?" The man frowned.

Gracie squinted at him. "Are you working for Wiley

Securities? Why the twenty-twenty questions?"

"Everything you do is important to me." Jason glared at her. "You are in some sort of trouble, aren't you?"

"No." Gracie scowled. "Why don't you leave?"

Jason frowned. "You were the one who showed up at my workplace crying, Gracie. You told me you needed to feel desirable. You brought me back here with you and then attacked me like a wild animal. Not that I am complaining. I like your wild side, but when you act this way you are in some sort of trouble."

"Shut up." Gracie turned away and headed to her living room. She started pacing. Jason was right. She was in trouble. She was in deep trouble. Maybe she hadn't thought the whole situation through, but who could have predicted that Saint would be so determined to reconcile with Sandrene.

She had been horrible to him the last couple of months, especially after he had refused to sleep with her.

How could he tell that she wasn't her sister? She had gotten everything right—Sandrene's perfume, Sandrene's walk, Sandrene's talk, and Saint still kept her at arm's length.

"Okay, I am going." Jason was now fully dressed. He paused at the door. "I am only going because I have a huge case tomorrow and I need my wits about me, but if you want me to stay..."

"No," Gracie inhaled raggedly, "It's the twenty-first century; we scratched an itch. Now go."

"Okay." Jason shook his head. "Slam, bam, thank you sir. This is cold, even for you. I know something is bothering you."

"I am fine."

"That's a lie," Jason looked at her with hooded eyes. "You know where to find me if you want to talk, have another itch to scratch, or want to feel desirable again..."

Gracie got up and brushed past him and opened the door.

Jason sighed. "When are you going to start trusting me, Gracie. I would literally do anything for you. Call me when you are ready. I am always waiting."

Gracie locked the door and then curled up on the settee. How had things gotten so desperately wrong? How did her perfect plan derail to this point?

She had thought that acting as her boring sister would have solved her problems. She had thought that it would be seamless, stepping into her sister's life, and living like her and getting all the things she had always envied Sandrene for, but nothing had gone as planned. Nothing was as she thought it would be.

The Waterfalls was not easy to run, there were a million and one decisions that she had to personally make that made things a bit overwhelming. On the home front, Saint was not a perfect husband. It's either Sandrene was lying, or Gracie's idea of perfect was way off.

She had never managed to recreate any of the perfect moments that her sister had written in her diary. To make things worse, Saint had refused to touch her.

Saint had been suspicious of her since day one and had refused to sleep with her. He had kissed her and had pulled back like a scalded cat. She had naively thought after she got rid of Sandrene that he wouldn't be able to distinguish between them.

So how could Saint tell the difference?

The question baffled her, kept her up at night. She acted like Sandrene. It had taken some effort to be peppy and bright all the time, but she had successfully pulled it off at first, but Saint was not buying it. While her face and behavior said Sandrene, there was something that yelled Gracie to Saint.

What was it?

She went searching in Sandrene's diaries for answers. Was there some special move that her sister had, some special scent? Some invisible chemical formula that Saint was reacting to?

After two months in, she hadn't cared anymore. She desperately wanted Saint to love her as Gracie though she was masquerading as Sandrene. To be honest, she still did, but her self-esteem had taken a battering.

She hated being rejected. She hated feeling undesirable. She hated to think that Sandrene was good at something she wasn't.

Saint had succeeded in pushing her away. Her last brilliant idea was to have him think that Sandrene no longer wanted the marriage. If she couldn't get him to love her, she was going to break them up.

It would make her feel better salve a little bit of her self-confidence if she were to mess up Sandrene's life.

She was already doing that at the restaurant. The employees at the restaurant were suspicious of her too.

Chef Brown, the head chef was calling her Gangrene Sandrene, and the rest of the staff had taken the name up. He had always been a perceptive bastard.

Gracie grimaced. He acted as if he owned the place. How dare he dictate to her that she either get her act together or he was going to quit?

"Argh," Grace pulled off her wig and flung it across the room. It bounced on a chair and settled at the door in a pool of fiber.

She hated this. How could she have thought to carry through with it?

All of this madness would have been bearable if Saint had treated her as a lover instead of a pariah, but he had the gall to reject her over and over again.

It was soul-crushing, but she wasn't so crushed that she wouldn't try again.

She wanted Saint to love her, and she wanted to prove that she could get the business to work like a well-oiled machine, and maybe she could still get those two desires.

She thought about what finally pushed her to be in this position. She closed her eyes.

****

Six months earlier...

It was a family meeting in the conference room at the Waterfalls. The place was soundproofed and had air conditioning and looked out on a mini courtyard that had a few points of interest like a wall to ceiling waterfall and a variety of glossy green plants that was maintained by the garden staff.

Sandrene was as usual neatly turned out in a black business suit; Gracie was dressed similarly but only because she was trying to be more like her sister.

It was working. Sanya looked between the two of them and frowned.

"What is going on?"

"What do you mean?" Gracie asked in her best Sandrene modulated voice.

Sanya shook her head. "What are you up to, Gracie? You hate modest business suits. Most of the times you prefer to dress as if you are going to a party."

"I am not up to anything, Mother," Gracie said cheekily.

"Yes, you are." Sanya swung her gaze to Sandrene. "Doesn't it bother you that she is acting like you? Dressing like you?

Wearing her hair the same? I can barely tell you two apart, and I am your mother."

"It doesn't bother me." Sandrene smiled. "I like this new Gracie. We are more like sisters now."

Sanya snorted but declined to comment.

Gracie narrowed her eyes at her mother. "I know what you are thinking. You think that I can't be like your precious Sandrene."

"You can't," Sanya said, "because you are my precious Gracie."

"You don't think I am precious," Gracie snorted. "I have always been your headache, the child that you wish you never had."

Lamar cleared his throat and looked at his watch. "Let us not segue into a petty argument about favorites. We have something important to discuss."

"This is not petty. My feelings should be heard, but because it's me, then its petty. In the order of things in this family. Sanjay is first, Sandrene is second, the Waterfalls is third, the grandchildren-Liam and Logan fourth and fifth. I am a distant last."

Gracie glared at both her parents. "I can be just like Sandrene. She is my twin."

"In face but not personality," Sanya said quickly, "but that is fine. We appreciate you for who you are, Gracie. Every child has their positives."

"Really?" Gracie snorted, "What is mine?"

Lamar sighed. "Gracie, I thought you outgrew this years ago."

"Outgrew what? The need for love and acceptance from my own family?" Gracie scowled. "I don't think so, Dad. I am never good enough for either of you. I am the best event planner this business has ever had. I bring in more dollars than Sandrene. It is my connections that propelled your little obscure restaurant to be the 'it' place."

"Come on, Gracie! We were never obscure. Your mother and I built this business for the past twenty-five years. Yes, your event planning added some value, but Sasha was doing a great job before she moved on."

"Some value..." Gracie widened her eyes angrily. "I brought in five celebrity weddings in a year. This is now the 'it' place to dine and to marry and it is all because of me. You are all crazy if you think that my value is negligible. I am making this place money hand over fist."

Sanya sighed and looked at her husband. "And that brings us to the reason for this meeting. We are going to Australia for a year."

"What?" Gracie rolled her eyes. "Let me guess. The first child… your favorite child crooked his finger, and you guys just had to run to help Sanjay who can't do anything without his mommy and daddy. That leaves you with the second favorite Sandrene, who is going to run the Waterfalls in your absence. How am I doing so far?"

"Pretty accurate." Sanya nodded. "Except we do not have favorites, and you know that. Sanjay needs help to start up a restaurant in Melbourne. We have the experience, and we want to see our grandchildren, they grow up so fast. We think it is the perfect opportunity to take a much-needed vacation in a new place. We have never taken such a long vacation from the restaurant, and we believe that Sandrene is capable of holding things down for us until we get back."

Gracie tapped her fingers on the table mutinously and then glared at her parents and Sandrene.

Obviously, Sandrene was not surprised by the revelation. She was observing the exchange with interest, not saying much because they had previously discussed it as a family.

This was just the 'reveal it' to Gracie session. Just as they did everything else. They handled her with care as if she was a volatile person. They had never gotten past her rebellious teenage years or the fact that she was not a conformer like Sanjay and Sandrene. Her parents did not like different, and she marched to her own beat. She was too out there for them. Too liberal for their conservative tastes.

Gracie growled. "I can run this place just as well as Sandrene, even better."

"We were hoping that you would work together." Sanya sighed. "Gracie, please do not be a beast about this, or turn this into a petty sibling competition. Your sister will need your support."

Gracie nodded, swallowing back her anger. "Oh, she'll get it. Let it not be said that I am not cooperative. I can act just like Sandrene, just watch me."

She wanted to storm out of the room with her head held high, righteous indignation in her wake, but she didn't. That was what they expected of her, but she wasn't going to indulge them.

Instead, she stayed in the conference room, nodding and smiling at the appropriate places listening to their banter as they blew off the conversation as if it were over, but she was fuming.

How dare they imagine that she was some sort of dimwit, that she couldn't run the place? How dare they think that Sandrene was better than her, had a better life, made better decisions.

They were identical for crying out loud. She would show them.

She stayed behind long after they had left, drumming the pen on the table seething about the situation.

She had a one o'clock appointment with a couple who was

going to have a reception on Saturday night, and she should be concentrating on planning for the event, but she couldn't.

How hard would it be to get rid of Sandrene?

Not kill her, make her disappear. She was many things, but a murderer wasn't one of them, but she wanted Sandrene out of her life. She wanted space and distance between them; she didn't want to be overshadowed by her anymore.

"Excuse me, Miss Russell," Gracie looked up. It was the gardener, Benjamin. "They told me no one would be in here. I have to attend to the plants in the courtyard."

Gracie waved him on and then paused to admire his retreating back. He was good looking. He would have warranted a second glance if he wasn't on staff. Her parents had a no fraternizing with the staff rule.

The rule was made because of her, and she had to admit grudgingly that it was warranted.

She had a fling with one of the waiters in the past. He had a girlfriend who had come to the restaurant to confront her with a machete.

The girl had created a big commotion the likes of which Gracie had never seen. She had genuinely feared for her life. Luckily, the security guard had intervened, or she would be without a limb right now or possibly even her neck.

Maybe she did cause her parents grief. It was not easy living up to their values and attitudes, and they hated when she did her own thing. She hadn't blamed them when they had practically kicked her out of their house earlier this year and bought a fixer upper place for her on the other side of town.

Of course, they had pretended that they just happened to get her a place for her birthday, but they had been tired of her living with them, and they had wanted her as far from them as possible.

Sandrene lived closer to them. Gracie grimaced. Of course, Sandrene had to be the one with the handsome husband, who had a close-knit family of brothers who were so deliciously handsome it was unreal.

If she were Sandrene, she would sample them all.

"Are you hurt, Mama?" The gardener's voice intruded on her reverie. "What's a memory inhibitor?

"You have to put it back. Mama, they are powerful drugs. What are you going to do with them?"

Gracie forgot her musings and strained her ears to hear more.

But Benjamin's voice kept getting lower and lower. He glanced at her furtively when he finally hung up the phone, and she pretended as if she hadn't pulled her chair even closer to the window to eavesdrop.

Gracie's curiosity was more than piqued. She watched him as he finished watering and polishing the plants.

She pounced when he was walking through the conference room.

"What's wrong with your mother, Benjamin? And what has she stolen."

"Miss Russell," Benjamin paused and then looked at her guiltily. "It was nothing."

"Spare me the lies." Gracie looked at him assessingly. "All it would take is one phone call, and I'll know who your mother is, where she works..."

Benjamin swallowed. "Miss Russell."

"Please call me Sandrea or Gracie." Gracie folded her hands under her chin. "I don't care which one. Miss Russell sounds so formal."

"Well Gracie," Benjamin cleared his throat. "I er...that was my mother. She works in a research facility in St. Mary. There was a fire, and she decided to save some things. I told her to give them back."

"What kind of drug did she steal?" Gracie narrowed her eyes at him. "She wasn't buying the 'save' some things argument."

"She saved them not steal them," Benjamin sighed. "The drug doesn't have a name yet. It is still in the development stages."

"I heard you say something about a memory inhibitor?" Gracie smiled, piling on the charm. "Come on Benjamin I am not your enemy just trying to offer a listening ear."

Benjamin grimaced, and half turned away. "I... ah, should get going. I have the front gardens to do."

Gracie picked up her cell phone. "No, you don't. I am calling my mom. I am going to have you fired."

Benjamin widened his eyes. "Why? I didn't do anything."

"You are insubordinate, refusing to answer my questions. I thought the Waterfall paid well, but obviously, you have a couple of other jobs lined up."

"No, I don't." Benjamin looked at her mutinously. "I need the money. I am buying a piece of property in Limestone Hill where I am from."

"Limestone Hill," Gracie snorted, "never heard of it."

"That's because it is very rural. We don't have electricity or running water. There isn't even a proper road to go there. It's pretty though, and so green, and the land is fertile."

Gracie smirked. "How much does this fertile land cost?"

"Two hundred and fifty thousand." Benjamin glared at her. "Why do you ask?"

"That's less than what I pay for my credit card bills every month," Gracie said contemplatively. "How much land is it?"

"Five acres," Benjamin growled. "Miss Gracie, I don't see what this has to do with anything."

"I'll give you the money if you tell me what I want to hear."

"What?" Benjamin gasped.

"What did your mother steal?"

"She said they were doing... ah... what's it called? Clinical trials, the drugs are supposed to make people forget things."

"As in amnesia?" Gracie widened her eyes. "Chemical amnesia? Wow. I had no idea they had that kind of scientific research going on in Jamaica."

"It is an independent lab. Some local and overseas doctors are working together. They want to take advantage of the local herbs and stuff." Benjamin shrugged. "My mother is going to give back the drugs. I don't know why she would take it anyway; it has no use to her or anyone. Who would want to forget unless they had some kind of trauma in their lives or something?"

Gracie rubbed her chin. "I have use for it."

"You do?" Benjamin frowned. "But why. Your life is perfect."

"My whole life is traumatic. Being born a twin is especially traumatic for me." Gracie grinned widely. "Can I speak to your mother? I need to know how it works."

"But it's not even on the market yet, it is stolen goods," Benjamin said worriedly, "and my mother doesn't know anything she is not a doctor she is just a janitor. I wish you never heard the conversation."

Sandrene chose that moment to stick her head through the door. "Hey Gracie, your one o'clock is here. Should I send them in?"

She then looked across at Benjamin and smiled.

Sandrene was so sickeningly sweet, Gracie thought resentfully. She was sweet to everybody as if she were in a Miss Congeniality contest.

"Hey, Benjamin. How is it going."

"Hi, Sandy." He responded like a lovesick crack-head, and

it hadn't escaped her notice that they were on a first name basis. He had called her Miss Russell, and he was calling her sister Sandy!

"Yes, send them in here, Sandrene." Gracie waited until Sandrene left before she looked at Benjamin knowingly. "You and I are not done, Benjamin, if you want that five acres of land, that is."

Benjamin dithered at the door. "Miss Russell...Gracie, I don't want to get mixed up in anything illegal."

"Illegal?" Gracie pretended innocence. "Oh no, never. What's your mother's name and number? She and I should have a chat. Maybe she'll want the money instead. Mother's usually know what is best for their sons."

"Her name is Angie Larson." Benjamin paused. "Her phone does not work in Limestone Hill where she lives, no cell phone signal. She is going back there today."

"Nice try," Gracie chuckled. "She isn't gone yet. She just called you. Give me her number, or you are fired, and I'll let the police know what you two are up to."

Chapter Eight

Limestone Hill, St. Mary-Four months ago

"**W**hat are you doing?" Miss Angie bellowed from the kitchen door.

"I...I... was trying to draw water from the tank," Sandrene stammered, as she stared wide-eyed at the wiry frame of her mother-in-law.

"Look here," Miss Angie advanced to the side of the brown cement well that was used as a water tank. "Take the drawing pan," she pointed at the pan as Sandrene still looked clueless, it was an ordinary plastic ice-cream bucket that had a rope attached to its handle.

"Beat away the water like so." She demonstrated to Sandrene the gentle swaying of her hands as the moss on top of the water parted by the gentle gliding of the bucket. "When you see an opening dip the bucket."

She flicked her wrist expertly, and the bucket dipped under

the water. She pulled up the full bucket, the water barely sloshing over the side. She did it so effortlessly her body hardly reflecting the effort.

Sandrene leaned at the side of the concrete tank, her hands folded. She stared unseeingly past the slightly moss-covered top to the june plum trees in the background.

This was rural living at its worst, and something did not feel right about the setup. She didn't feel right. This whole scenario felt as foreign to her as if somebody had plucked her from reality and into a nightmare as if she was still in a dream.

She kept hoping that she would wake up, but she couldn't.

She remembered her childhood, her teen years, but the rest of it was blank darkness.

Gracie had told her that she had been in an accident. She had fallen off a bike in spin class at the gym and had bumped her head hard on the bike next to her.

She rubbed her neck area. It felt tight and tense, and there was a big knot there. Was it so easy to lose memories, though? Just from a fall?

She looked into the moss-covered water again. She was married to Benjamin Larson, a man that felt like a total stranger. He looked vaguely familiar, that was a plus, but there had been no recognition of him as her husband.

Sandrene didn't remember their wedding. She didn't remember anything. Whole chunks of her life were missing. She had to rely on her twin sister, Gracie to fill in the blanks but Gracie said he was her husband. According to Gracie, she had been married for close to a year.

A year! A quiet wedding in the registrar's office. Why a quiet wedding without her parents around?

It didn't sound much like her.

Lots of things didn't sound like how she thought life

would turn out. She was twenty-five, had gotten a Culinary Management degree but since her parents had fallen on hard times and closed the restaurant, she was between jobs.

Gracie, on the other hand, was married and was running her own event planning business.

Sandrene winced at the pain that shot across her brow as she struggled to remember. She couldn't recall a thing past her high school graduation dinner. Her parents had thrown quite a party, and she had felt guilty because Gracie had not graduated. It had made her feel odd that her twin was not feted and celebrated as well.

She wished her parents had been around to confirm all of this, but according to Gracie, they were gone to Australia for a year after they had closed the restaurant and the number that Gracie gave her to call was perpetually busy. They didn't have cell phone service where they were according to Gracie, much like where she was now.

Sandrene massaged the back of her neck. The uncomfortable feeling that a key puzzle piece was missing from her life haunted her. This whole countryside felt like she had stepped into an alternate reality. The whole story about her parents closing their restaurant and moving to Australia was slightly absurd.

And why had Gracie and Benjamin sneaked her out of the medical center like a fugitive on the run?

Benjamin had insisted that they needed to come back here to this place as soon as possible because they had business to take care of. Gracie had waved her off with her bags in hand with a smug, mission accomplished smile on her face. Sandrene had learned not to trust that smile. Whenever Gracie wore that smile things were about to get nasty.

Gracie wasn't answering her questions as it related to her and Benjamin, at least not in a way that was satisfactory to her.

She wanted to know why she married Benjamin and moved to this very rural part of the country?

And why Benjamin?

Gracie had said he was a wealthy farmer who did business with the restaurant and Sandrene had lost her head over him and decided to get married. Just like that.

But in the last couple of days, since Sandrene woke up in the medical center, she had looked at Benjamin and felt nothing.

Nothing at all.

He had been there for her though, looking at her with such concern in his eyes that she was convinced he cared about her. When she first opened her eyes at the medical center, she saw him praying at the side of her bed.

"Please God, let her be alive. I beg you."

She had felt nothing on seeing him, but she thought that with her memories gone her emotions had taken a hiatus as well. If she had recently married, how is it that she felt nothing for her new husband? He wasn't bad looking. He was tall with an athletic build and good looking, in a clean-cut kind of way. He was polite and sweet when he spoke, but he didn't say much.

They had taken a bus to Limestone Hill just a day ago after she had woken up in the medical center. Benjamin said they needed to leave the city because he needed to go home to work on the farm.

She had to haul her bags for miles until hot and disheveled and hopping on one leg they reached a place in the mountains that defied description.

They were in the middle of nowhere. Every now and then they would see little board houses with smoke spiraling from the backyards, but then the foliage would get thick again, and the house would disappear from view.

"Where are we?" she had managed to choke out, as her face dripped with sweat.

"Near the farm," was Benjamin's surprisingly timid answer. He had gotten more and more subdued when they alighted the bus and was determinedly silent as they trekked the broken track to the woodlands.

They had finally reached a particularly weather-beaten board house with numerous trees in the front yard when Benjamin stopped. There was a track that led to the front step which Sandrene could see from the road was dyed in red.

"Ehem...Sandrene...I," Benjamin had opened his mouth to speak and then shifty-eyed he looked away.

"Where is this, Benjamin?" Sandrene asked him puzzled.

"This is my mother's house." He looked around and seemed to sigh with relief. "It seems as if she is not home. She sells at the market sometimes. Especially since she is no longer working in the town."

"Why don't we just go to your house? I am tired, and these bags are heavy."

"Sandy we ah ...we will be staying here until my farmhouse gets repaired I had some minor damages."

"Oh... Okay," Sandrene dragged her legs to the small dwelling. Her eyes taking in the rotting boards that enclosed the verandah and the multi-colored zinc that sloped down to form a rain gutter at the front of the house.

Her head was beginning to throb.

"Benjamin this is small," she looked back at him as she tentatively sat on one of the low benches on the verandah.

"Well, it has two bedrooms, a hall, and an outside bathroom and kitchen."

Sandrene felt her head start to spin.

"I am not using an outside bathroom, Benjamin" she felt a roar in her veins, "I don't care what repairs have to be done on your house, I am going. Where is it?"

She got up to leave.

Benjamin sat on the bench facing hers; the verandah suddenly seemed crowded.

"I lied, Sandy."

"Lied about what? The repairs?" Sandrene sat down hard on the bench, her mouth opened. She hated when he called her Sandy, and she didn't know why.

Before Benjamin could speak, a tall, middle-aged woman with a straw basket in her hands came walking down the path.

"Benjy! I heard you were here." Her voice carried down the walkway, and she walked faster to meet Benjamin, who got up from the bench and went to greet her.

She enfolded him in a hug, her tall frame almost the same height as he was. Her face was suffused with motherly pleasure as she looked at him critically.

"Welcome home, boy," she suddenly realized that Sandrene was there and asked, "Is this her?"

"Yes Mama, this is my wife, Sandrene" Benjamin gestured in Sandrene's direction.

To say his mother was speechless was an understatement. Her mouth was shaped in an O and then she smiled revealing a gap in the front of her mouth.

"You were right, she is pretty, very pretty and so sophisticated looking." she nodded at Sandrene shyly. "My name is Miss Angie, that's what everybody calls me here. "Come, come let me show you where you sleep. She led the way into the cramped house.

Sandrene was shown to a bedroom that had two single beds that were separated by a dilapidated chest of drawers with marks along the wood surface. Next door to that was the hall and then another bedroom that was furnished in the same manner.

"This is where you will stay." Miss Angie pointed to the back bedroom. "The kitchen and bathroom are outside, and we eat on the verandah or in the hall." She pointed to the dinghy hall that had a chair and an old sofa that looked as if it was once red.

Sandrene could see that poverty was stamped on the house. The back bedroom had holes in the boards; those were stuffed with newspaper.

Why didn't Benjamin take his mother to live with him in his big farmhouse with the view of the river that he told her about? He told her he had six bedrooms and six bathrooms and yet he had his mother living in squalor.

It was an outrage.

Before Sandrene could voice her thoughts, Miss Angie interrupted her.

"That is your lamp." She pointed to a home sweet home lamp.

"What do you mean?" Sandrene asked puzzled.

"We don't have current, as in electricity," Miss Angie said. "This is not like your fancy Kingston. This is very rural St Mary. You'll need the lamp to see at nights. When the oil runs out, Benjamin will buy more."

"Oh, we won't be here that long," Sandrene smiled at Miss Angie. "Benjamin's house repairs won't take us that long. We'll be out of your hair before you know it."

Miss Angie looked at Sandrene weirdly and then shook her head. "Benjamin's house?" She asked incredulously. "Where did you…?"

"Mama," Benjamin walked over to his mother. "How is Carlene?"

"Who is Carlene?" Sandrene looked between the two of them inquisitively.

"Carlene is my daughter." Miss Angie smiled. "She lives on the other side of the hill. She has given me three wonderful grandchildren. I assume that you will soon be breeding too. It will be good to have some grandchildren with the Larson surname. My husband, God rest his soul was a good man."

Sandrene shuddered at the coarse way that she said 'breed' and went into the little dusty room to sit on the bed.

She closed her eyes, and the image of dark green eyes and brown curly hair came to mind. She tried to hang on to the thought, but it escaped her.

"Sandrene," Miss Angie clutched the drawing pan, bringing her back to the present. "I won't be drawing water for you every time you need it, so you have to learn."

"I won't need to," Sandrene stood over the tank and gazed at the green looking liquid in its depths. "Benjamin's house is about to be fixed, and we will soon be out of here."

Miss Angie started to laugh. "That is not anytime soon, my love. First, he has to build a house for it to be fixed." She then headed into the kitchen to deposit the water into another ice cream bucket that was chipped and scraped along the rim.

Sandrene followed her to the dark little zinc building that they called 'the kitchen.' It was square soot-stained room, pots hung from little hooks and nails in the dark interior. There were two pudding pans that held water, a dishwashing liquid bottle sat beside it on a table. It smelled of seasoning, and Sandrene realized that onions and garlic were hanging from a string in the rafters of the room. A coal pot sat in one corner with a black sack of coal beside it.

"Would you like a drink?" Miss Angie asked politely as she watched how Sandrene tried to contain a shudder.

"You have a refrigerator?" Sandrene asked relieved, looking around.

"Course I do," Miss Angie bent down to an igloo in the corner and grabbed a soft drink that was sitting on ice and handed it to Sandrene.

"Thanks," Sandrene said taking the soft drinks as if it were going to bite her. The irony had not escaped her, and she was sure that Miss Angie was silently laughing at her expense.

"The ice comes from Mister Lukey shop 'round the corner. He has a gas operated freezer. When this ice melts out, one of us will have to go for more."

"What?" Sandrene exclaimed with such force that Miss Angie who was on the verge of sifting through a coal bag that was in the corner stopped suddenly.

"I think we have to share the work around here," Miss Angie said angrily. "I have no idea why Benjamin had to leave and go clear to Kingston to find a wife, but when he is gone to the farm in the days, you and I will have to share the work. This is no hotel, and I am no babysitter, ask my daughters they know that."

Sandrene waited until Miss Angie finished her tirade and with narrowed eyes, she asked quietly, "What exactly am I to do as Benjamin's wife?"

She felt hot and sticky, and even though the mountain air was cool, she felt a heat bubbling up inside waiting to be released.

"Well for starters," Miss Angie said with her hands akimbo. "I expect you to help with the cooking."

"You mean come in here and cook?" Sandrene asked incredulously. "I have not been here two hours, and yet you want me to help with the cooking?"

"Not today, you can start tomorrow."

"Go on," Sandrene replied, tightening her hands around

the soft drink can.

"To wash Benjamin's farm clothes."

"Surely Benjamin doesn't go on the farm himself," Sandrene replied, "he delegates."

"Dele-what?" Miss Angie replied. "The man works on a farm," she continued staring at the innocent face of her fake daughter-in-law. "He digs yam and plants cassava and dasheen and cabbage then I bring it to market to sell.

You can help with the selling, some mornings the basket gets too heavy with the onions and things. The donkey that we borrow from Charles is very slow, so you can carry the basket and start selling in the market till I arrive with more produce."

Sandy stood mutinously, her brain trying to wrap around this newest bit of information.

She must have nodded because Miss Angie continued. "When you are washing Benjamin's clothes, you will have to go to the river because the tank is only quarter full right now, and according to Mother Pansy, who knows when the rain is coming, we will not get rain till next week."

Sandrene realized that her fingers were digging into the side of the can and that soft drink was running down her fingers.

"Apart from that, you can go to the government pipe but that is one mile, and you'll have to hire Mister Jasper's push-cart. I am tired of telling lazy Benjy to make one so that we can do our own hauling."

"Oh, by the way," Miss Angie called out to Sandrene as she stumbled from the kitchen doorway. "Sometimes Carlene and her three children sleep over when her man kicks her out, so you and Benjamin will have to share the room."

Sandrene stumbled over to an ackee tree and sat down on a stone.

She had heard of poverty, but this was beyond poor. Her patchy memories brought up a privileged childhood in Kingston. She had the luxurious comforts of electricity and running water that came out of taps.

Her parents lived in a relatively large house in Beverly Hills.

They ran a restaurant called the... She groaned in frustration. She couldn't remember the name of the restaurant.

She looked around the yard. Obviously, she had no idea where she was or who she got married to. Benjamin must have swept her off her feet. She wondered about the face of the man she kept seeing when she closed her eyes. She felt a yearning for him that was a bit overwhelming.

Who was he? How did he fit into this picture?

She wiped the tears that were running unhindered down her face and went back to the gloomy doorway of the kitchen. Miss Angie had a good fire going, and she was humming as she stoked the coal pot.

"What was Benjamin doing in Kingston?" She asked Miss Angie aggressively.

Miss Angie stopped mid-hum and wiped her hands on an already black looking cloth.

"He was house-sitting for Mr. Blackwood, the man that owns the farm that he works on. Mr. Blackwood paid him to stay at the house and keep the place until his wife got back from England. He also worked as a gardener at a restaurant. They had a beautiful garden for weddings and such."

Sandrene heard a ringing in her ears. It was no wonder Benjamin was so careful not to tell her anything much about his so-called farm though she had peppered him with questions when they had made the long bus ride to this middle of nowhere.

"There isn't a six-bedroom house, is there?" Sandrene

asked wearily.

"I don't know what you are talking about, chile'" Miss Angie looked puzzled. "You keep referring to a house, but this is the only place that Benjamin could call his. You can't see it from here, but he plants the bottom side of the land with yam, cassava, cabbage, and bananas. He also works on Mr. Blackwood's farm as his handyman."

Sandrene was speechless. So, when he said that he was going to check on the farm, he was talking about Mr. Blackwood's farm.

Miss Angie sighed. "He didn't tell you, did he?"

Sandrene shook her head. "I don't know what's going on. This whole thing feels weird. I am not sure why I even married your son. When I close my eyes, I see someone else. This can't be my life."

She blinked back tears and then realized that she couldn't keep them away, not successfully. She started sobbing, her body wracked with grief.

Miss Angie hugged her to her bony chest. She seemed speechless herself.

"I had a happy childhood in Kingston," Sandrene choked out. "I don't know how I got here. I have no idea how I came to this. I need to call my sister or my parents. I need to go back. I shouldn't have come. I don't know why Gracie convinced me that this was the best thing to do. I…I am so sorry, Miss Angie. I can't stay here. This is not me."

She looked at Miss Angie with tear filled eyes. "This might sound shallow, but I can't live without a fridge and a flushable toilet. This place doesn't even have electricity."

Miss Angie nodded and soothed her. "Don't worry, chile. I'll fix it for you. Relax. when I am finished, everything will be OK."

Chapter Nine

Sandrene woke up in a tiny room. She was shivering under blankets, and a drum was beating outside. A man was sitting in a chair over her, his face was unshaven, and he looked haggard. He was handsome, in a rugged sort of way.

"Hello," she croaked. Her voice sounded ill-used, and she felt heavy as if her body wasn't hers.

He sat up suddenly, his bloodshot eyes focusing on her face.

"Thank God, I thought you were dead."

"Dead? What do you mean?"

"Those medications are powerful. Mama is now holding a session for you outside."

"Where is this?"

"Limestone Hill." He answered slowly.

" Who am I?"

"What are you saying, Sandy. Don't you remember anything?"

"My name is Sandy?" She tested the name on her tongue. "Sandy," she said louder.

She tried to sit up, and he helped her. She had on an old-fashioned nightgown with frills at the neck and sleeves. It was an ugly shade of pink.

"May I see myself in the mirror, please?" she asked as she looked around in the small cramped space of the room.

The man handed her a mirror, and she looked at the face staring back at her. She had a smooth toffee colored complexion. Her eyes were clear brown, and her hair was in tiny curls cut in a low style. She had a bump on her forehead that was the size of an egg.

"What happened to my head?" she looked at the man who was standing uncertainly near the bed.

"You don't remember anything at all?" He asked wonderingly.

"No," she frowned, "what happened to me?"

"Eh…er…er…you blocked out, and Mama found you. You hit your head. You block out a lot."

"Am I your sister?" Sandrene asked looking again at the stranger's face.

"No, I am your husband. My name is Benjamin."

"Oh, okay" she digested this for a while. "I have so many questions. My brain is like a blank slate. Where am I from? Where is this? What about my family?"

"You are from er…from… er…Savannalamar in Westmoreland."

Sandrene nodded.

"I met you at the market there," Benjamin added quickly. "We got married and came up here to live in St. Mary, Limestone Hill."

"What about my family?" Sandrene asked feeling uneasy. His answers were coming in spurts as if he was not sure.

"They are…they are…dead. And you were an only child."

"They are?" Sandrene's eyes filled with tears. "I don't have any mother, father or siblings?"

"No, you don't." Benjamin sighed. "My family is all you have now. We live with my mother, and you help her around the house, and sometimes at the market like what you used to do before in er...May Pen."

"May Pen?" Sandrene questioned, "I lived in May Pen too?"

"I meant Savannalamar," Benjamin mumbled. "You were only in May Pen a short while."

"Oh, why can't I remember a thing, Benjamin? Sandrene asked frustratedly.

"As I said, you hit your head. Try to relax. I guess when you do all the memories will come back."

"When did I hit my head?" Sandrene questioned,

"Two days ago," Benjamin ran his hand over his face. "Don't move. I am going to tell Mama that you are okay."

"Okay." Sandrene smiled at him. "How old am I? Just tell me that before you go."

"Twenty-four," this time he answered without hesitation. "You celebrated your birthday the other day. It was a nice occasion."

And it had been. Benjamin thought wistfully. Sandrene had given all the workers a gift. She believed that the birthday celebrant should be the gift giver and not the one receiving gifts. It was weird and quirky, but they all looked forward to her birthday.

She had thrown a party in the conference room. Saint was there looking on her proudly. He had even taken the time to speak to Benjamin, asking him how his farm was coming on.

She didn't deserve this. Benjamin closed the room door and leaned on it. This was unfair to her. They had injected her with the substance twice, and after a third time, they had wiped her memories. Probably damaging her brain forever.

It was an experimental drug; they didn't know the side effects. They didn't know anything. They could be killing her right now. This was wrong on so many levels; he shouldn't have allowed his mother and Gracie to talk him into this.

He shouldn't have collected the half a million dollars that Gracie had dangled in front of him like a carrot. How could he keep on lying to Sandrene? He wasn't a very good liar.

He went in search of his mother who was just closing her pocomania session. Her white dress was flapping behind her as she threw water at the four corners of the yard. She had her rituals. He didn't interfere, but he thought that splashing the yard and chanting was not the best thing to do in this situation. The best thing to do was take Sandrene back to her loving husband in Kingston and give back Gracie her blood money.

"Mama," Benjamin went out to her, keeping his voice down. "She's awake."

"I told you she would be," his mother said, continuing with her splashing.

"But Mama she has been sleeping for two days. How was I to know that you hadn't killed her with that injection? What kind of drug is this?"

"It has never killed anybody. At least not in the test trials. Did she have a memory of anything?"

"No, she didn't even remember her name. This drug is even more powerful than I thought. When Gracie gave it to her first, she had only forgotten a few months, the second time years, the third time, her childhood and now everything! This is dangerous, Mama, and I don't think that this is the way that they intended to use it. That's three injections in a matter of weeks."

"But it works," his mother sounded satisfied. "Now you have a blank slate to work with. Did you hide the pretty clothes that she carried with her?"

"Yes I did, they are in your room under your bed." Benjamin looked uncertain. "I am not sure this is the right thing to do, Mama. I was going to tell her the truth and take her back to Kingston."

"Are you mad?" His mother looked him over. "The girl was only half remembering things and was about to leave. I was not about to let her get away. In case you have not noticed, no woman in their right mind will come near you after that thing with the goat, Benjamin. You are ruined for life."

Benjamin opened his mouth to speak. "I was not …I am not…"

"Whether or not it was your intention, they caught you running after the goat with your pants down…" she frowned slightly, her voice trailing away.

"The goat stole my shirt," Benjamin said exasperatedly. "I had to run it down before it ate it. I was just coming out of the river, of course, I was naked."

"Nobody will believe that," his mother frowned. "You should be happy that nobody is talking anymore since they heard that you are married. All is forgiven, especially since I told them that she is a beautiful girl from a good family in May Pen."

"I told her she was from Savannalamar" Benjamin looked over his mother's head and into the falling dusk. When it got dark in the mountains, it was pitch dark. There was no hint of light for many miles, especially so when the moon wasn't out.

"Well, she doesn't have to know that this isn't so. She is like an open blank book. We can write whatever story we want in it." his mother sighed. "I told her everything, you know, about Mr. Blackwood and the fact that you did not have a house and she took it hard. I knew that I had to use the injection the moment I came out of the kitchen and saw her hanging over the tank. So, I told her anyway. I only have three left, though. I gave Gracie two and kept four. I hope this does not wear out of her system anytime soon."

"What about her family?" Benjamin asked. "They will be looking for her."

"I thought you said Gracie was acting as her," Miss Angie said. "Nobody in Kingston knows where Sandrene is, except for Gracie."

"No, but Gracie cannot act like Sandrene forever." Benjamin sighed. "This is wrong. I shouldn't have listened to Gracie. You know, when I worked for their family, Sandy was the nice one. She and Gracie were identical physically, but you could feel the difference in personality as soon as either of them opened their mouth."

"Forget all that," Miss Angie snorted, "wasn't Sandrene the one who you used to tell me about?"

"Yes," Benjy nodded.

"And wasn't she the one who broke your heart when she married this other man?"

"Yes, but I had no right to be heartbroken. I was just a gardener at their restaurant. I had a crush on her because she was nice to me. She was nice to everyone." Benjy rubbed his hand over his face. "Her husband, Saint Wiley, will kill me when he finds out my part in this. He is a karate expert. I once saw him chop three bricks with his hands."

"Magic trick." Miss Angie snorted.

"No, it wasn't." Benjamin held his head. "He is an expert in karate and kickboxing and whatever else, and he was in the army. I overheard his friend Max talking about him, and he said he was an expert marksman. Besides, he owns one of those security companies that do surveillance and intelligence and all those things. They have better resources than the government to fight crime. He is going to find us and kill me. Mama, I don't think this is worth it."

"Oh yes, it is worth it. Gracie paid us good money to do this. I have never had so much money hidden under my mattress."

"It's dirty money. I am thinking of giving it back."

"Oh no, you don't," Angie growled. "Half of it is mine."

"We have this money at the expense of what, Mama? What if we kill Sandrene? What would we do, just bury her at the bottom of the land and pretend that she didn't exist? We have no clue what is in that drug you keep giving her. It could happen. The last time it knocked her out for two days. What's in that injection anyway?"

"I may not know what is in it," Miss Angie sniffed, "but I heard Dr. Peters describing how it worked one night when I was cleaning. He was giving a presentation to some business types, and one man asked him to break it down in layman terms.

"Dr. Peters said that the injection suppresses memories, is fast acting and effective, and lasts three months currently, but they were working on a long-term solution.

"When the fire broke out at the research center there were six of them on the desk in the lab, all lined up in one of those clear glass trays. I grabbed them. God knew it would come in handy someday."

"God doesn't endorse this." Benjamin closed his eyes and bowed his head. "Mama I am not a criminal."

"You are just as much a criminal as me and Gracie Russell." Miss Angie cackled.

"No, I am not." Benjamin cleared his throat. "This is

wrong."

"If you are not a criminal," Miss Angie folded her arms and glared at him, "what would you call taking a woman who is not yours and telling her a pack of lies to keep her. You should count your blessings and move on. Instead of moping about right or wrong.

"As I said, I have three injections left, if what Dr. Peters said is right and they last three months, we have a year with her. Who knows, maybe she will want to stay after the effects of the thing wears off and fall in love with her life here."

"But suppose it kills her?" Benjamin asked troubled. "Suppose it messes up her head forever. Mama, I don't like this."

Benjamin went back into the house, the enormity of what they had done weighing on his mind.

But the joy that Sandrene could be his for a year was an exciting prospect. He had long admired her, and now she was his, a blank slate. He could have her for as long as it lasted.

And then what?

Jail, if Saint didn't catch him first, but he never would. Gracie was filling in for Sandy.

****

Sandrene woke up the next morning with a hand shaking her shoulder. "It's work time, gal."

A middle-aged lady in a multi-colored tie head was bending over her.

She straightened up when Sandrene opened her eyes. Sandrene realized that the woman was tall. Her head was only a couple of inches below the beams in the ceiling.

She felt better in her body than last night, but she still

could not remember a thing, except that she had a husband, and this was his mother.

"My name is Miss Angie," the lady said to her, as she observed the confusion in Sandrene's eyes.

"Okay," Sandrene whispered.

"Today we will go to our piece of land about a half mile from here, and we will be sowing gungo peas for the Christmas harvest."

"But it's still dark," Sandrene looked through the crack of the dirty windows.

"The sooner, the better, gal. It's already 5:00, next time I'll wake you at 4:30."

Miss Angie left the room, and Sandrene came from under the sheet the air was cool almost cold. She hurriedly donned the pants and long-sleeved shirt that was placed on the bed for her.

Where was Benjamin? She needed to bathe she could smell herself, and her hair was a sorry mess, and her mouth tasted foul.

"Miss Angie," Sandrene said when she stepped out into the dinghy hall "I need to bathe, comb my hair, and brush my teeth."

"We will do that when we get back," Miss Angie mumbled, "we will be back before ten."

Sandrene followed Miss Angie through the door and up the beaten track in front of the house she looked at the landscape for the first time. The trees stood like hulking monsters in the dark of the morning, and the air was cold.

Her teeth were chattering, and white frost formed when she took in a breath and blew it out. Sandrene felt in her bones that this was not something that she was used to. Why were her hands so soft and her nails so nicely manicured if she did such hard work? Even her toenails looked well groomed.

"Where is Benjamin?" She asked Miss Angie as she traipsed behind her down the hill.

"Mr. Blackwood is leaving for England, so he is gone to take instructions from him regarding the cows."

She assumed that Benjamin worked for Mr. Blackwood. At least the name Blackwood meant something to her, that was a positive in her blank mush of a brain.

Miss Angie slowed down as they neared some fencing. The posts were painted white, and they looked neat. The first sign of any order in the bushes Sandrene thought.

"This is the beginning of the Blackwood's land," Miss Angie pointed. "We won't be able to see even half of it because it extends to the sea on the south side."

"Wow," Sandrene said politely.

"He employs nearly all the district," Miss Angie said. "He gives us land to farm and lease and live. He's a nice man."

Sandrene nodded. She felt grubby and listless. She wanted a bath.

Just then they reached a spot where the land was covered in Acacia trees and tall grass. The grass was almost up to her face.

Miss Angie handed her a machete and chuckled. "We have cabbage growing on the other acre, but this piece needs subduing."

"It's a huge piece of property." Sandrene opened her eyes wide. She couldn't see the other side, and the grass was wet and more slippery the deeper they waded into the wilderness.

"But we can do it." Miss Angie grinned. "I am fifty-four, done this by myself year after year, it's nice to have company."

After a hot morning in the thicket, they went back up the hill. Sandrene's hands felt heavy, and they were throbbing.

She felt tired and weary. She broke all her nails, her face was itching, and her feet felt like lead. Miss Angie showed her to the tank when they returned to what she now considered home.

"That's the drawing pan," she pointed to a bucket. "I showed you how to do this already, and you said that you had something like this in Savannalamar." She indicated the tank.

A ghost of a smile crossed her face as Sandrene grappled with the bucket. The blisters on her palms needed treatment, but Sandrene was docilely doing everything she was told.

"This is your bath pan," Miss Angie indicated a chipped blue pan and hauled it at the foot of the tank. "Everybody bathes out there." She pointed to a tree that had a piece of board at the bottom and planks that were nailed cross-wise at waist height.

"Put the pan on the plank and stand up on the board."

She left to go into the house, and Sandrene battled with the pan. She was drawing water with little green moss floating on the surface, her mind recoiled at this, but she pressed on anyway. Benjamin said she had no family left and so this was where she would be living for the rest of her life.

She shuddered at the thought. She was not comfortable. At the back of her mind, she felt that there was something more. She carried the bath pan with water splashing over the side to the tree. Her back strained at the unfamiliar weight, but she gratefully put down the pan and found a piece of soap on the plank she quickly stripped her clothes and used the rag that Miss Angie had silently handed to her earlier. It felt good against her body. She felt as if she hadn't bathed in days.

"You should wash your hair," Miss Angie called from the back door. "I have the hot combs ready to straighten it for you."

"I don't want it straightened, thank you," Sandrene said with certainty.

Miss Angie nodded. "Suit yourself. You have nice hair, but it looks like it could use a combing."

Sandrene washed her hair and put on fresh clothes. She felt new again.

Miss Angie indicated to a chair that was at the back of the house for her to sit. Sandrene hesitated. I am not sure about this.

"Don't worry. I do my daughters hair all the time. I have the oil and the gel. She held up two jars. I can give you some pretty finger coils. You have the hair for it."

Sandrene sat reluctantly.

Miss Angie ran her fingers through her curls and sighed. You have my daughter's Carlene kind of hair. She keeps hers short as well. She can't be bothered with long hair. It fits her face like yours does too. Not everybody can carry off a short hairstyle.

"I couldn't do it. My head is too square and bumpy."

Sandrene chuckled.

"That's what they used to call me in primary school, square head, Angie."

Miss Angie sighed. "Benjamin got lucky with you. You are a pretty girl. Very pretty. I'll have to keep an eye on you when we go to the market. They are like jackals out there, these men. I was so sorry I lost the job at the Research Center. It was easier. Loads easier than this farm and market business. I had the job for five years and then poof just like that they laid off everyone, excluding the doctors and moved to the Kingston. The place was not even burnt to the ground. Just a little fire and they got scared. Those doctors are wusses."

"The Research Center?" Sandrene asked.

"Yes," Miss Angie snorted, "I worked for a scientific research place in Port Maria."

" Kingston," Sandrene murmured. "Have I ever been to Kingston?"

"I doubt that, chile." Miss Angie finished up silently and handed Sandrene a mirror. Her hair was transformed into little ringlets that fell around her ears and forehead. They hid the scar near her hairline. It looked good. It looked familiar. A strong certainty gripped her that she had not only heard about Kingston, but she had been there, lived there.

"I have been to Kingston!" Sandrene said putting down the mirror.

"What did you say?" Miss Angie snapped.

"I remember Kingston. I have been there.

"What else do you remember?" Miss Angie growled.

"Nothing." Sandrene looked in Miss Angie's face. Somehow, she sensed that Miss Angie could not be trusted, not with her new memories. She would never mention remembering anything again.

Miss Angie did not look pleased; she got up and went into the house muttering.

Sandrene sat in the chair for a very long time trying hard to remember. She rubbed her forehead absently. Why couldn't she remember?

Chapter Ten

Present Day- August

Monday. A steady rainfall hammered the pavement outside the window. It was the kind of weather that Saint used to revel in, but not today. He felt heavy inside like a sack of luggage was sitting on his chest.

It didn't take a genius to know that he was in the throes of a depression. It didn't take much to guess why.

Sandrene was on his mind. He thought of her more, now that she was out of the house and playing independent woman than he did when they were living together.

He swung his chair to the parking lot view and watched as one by one his employees drove in and parked. At the same time, others from the control room staff who had worked the night shift drove out.

He had a meeting in thirty minutes with his top managers, and he was wondering how he should approach it. The meeting would confirm to his colleagues that his marriage was on the rocks because he would be using up significant manpower to watch his wife. It was not something that he was looking forward to saying out loud.

As Pastor Tate liked to say, he was speaking things to life. He had already told his brothers and sister-in-law, but this was taking it to a whole other level.

Of course, he could do it off the books and pay the security personnel personally. He could act like he was a client but to do that he would have to go through his Customer Relations Manager, Tom Briskett and then Briskitt would report it to Max Harry, his Operations Manager who would make a call to Keena Leslie his general manager, who would then call Matthew Blackwood the business development manager who would barge into his office and ask him what was going on.

It was just easier to meet with his three top managers, tell them what he wanted and have them deal with it.

After five years the business had settled into a well-oiled machine with a formal organizational structure.

He was chairman and owner of the company with a forty percent share in the business; the Wiley Group owned thirty percent, Matthew, Max, and Keena owned ten percent each.

When he was floating the idea for investment round in his security venture, the Wiley Group had readily bankrolled him. Max had wanted in; he preferred the administrative side of the security industry especially after their army training. Keena Leslie had been the general manager of a security company before but had been fired from the company when her ex-husband arranged for her to lose the job.

Saint had met Keena at church after Walter had introduced them.

Keena had been thinking of starting up a similar business

but didn't have the capital. She had been eager to buy into Wiley Security from the ground up. She had been a Godsend. She came with a whole portfolio of wealthy clients who needed their business, and she came with over twenty years of experience in the security industry.

Keena had saved them from years of struggling. They had bypassed the sluggish years of a startup and had hit the ground running.

In the first year, they had even made a profit. It was unheard of in a new venture. The parent company never had a need to bail them out, not even when they were in expansion mode, and he owed that to Keena.

Keena was now a staple in their lives and also a good friend of Sandrene's. Sandrene was her surrogate daughter since her two girls lived and worked in the British Virgin Islands.

Saint sighed. Keena had asked him a couple of weeks ago what was wrong with Sands, as Keena affectionately called his wife, but he did not know how to answer her.

And then there was Matthew Blackwood, his former college roommate. Matthew was a rich kid whose grandparents had left him a modest inheritance. He was a business whiz and the logical choice as his second in command.

They had practically planned the business venture together when they were in college. Matthew had been the first one to invest. Even before the Wiley Group.

What Saint liked most about his team was that they all had a vested interest in seeing the business succeed. In the third year of the business, he had taken off to England for six months of training but had no need to worry about losing it all when he got back.

He spent the six months in London with Sandrene. He did lots of business but had even more pleasure.

He wanted that time back. He wanted the time when he couldn't get enough of her when seeing her didn't fill him with indifference. He wanted to succeed at marriage. He made a success of everything else.

"Hey Saint," Matthew walked into his office with a stack of papers in his hand. "Can we talk before the meeting?"

"Sure." Saint snapped back into business mode. He was not a moper. It was time to cease the day, run the company that he loved and concentrate on everything else but Sandrene.

"Why do you come to work earlier than I do?" Saint asked his friend. "Don't tell me you have wife troubles too?"

Matthew looked at him sharply. "No, wife troubles. Abby and I are fine. She went to the country for the weekend; her cousin had a bachelorette party, girls only."

Saint nodded. "That's good to know."

"What's going on with you and Sandrene?" Matthew raised an eyebrow.

"She moved out. I wanted to discuss that in the meeting today when Max and Keena get here. I want her watched and I want a thorough investigation of everything that she has been up to in the past four months."

Matthew nodded. "Cool. Abby did mention that Sandrene was er..."

"What?" Saint frowned.

"Acting like a..." Matthew swallowed. "I would rather not say the words. I couldn't believe it. Abby went to the restaurant for their regular Tuesday meet up a couple of weeks ago, and she said Sandrene completely blanked her, treated her as if she didn't know her and told her to stop bothering her while she was working."

Saint steepled his fingers under his chin. "Interesting."

"Yes," Matthew sighed, "glad to get that off my chest. I didn't want to bring it up. I know how people get when they hear about their loved ones acting weird."

"Weird is the word." Saint sighed. "Everybody who knows us is commenting on it. She said she wants a divorce."

"Goodness." Matthew groaned. "I thought you two would last. You have always been committed to each other. Abby and I look up to you guys. You both gave us hope that young couples can go the long haul. I hate to see you giving up on a good thing."

Saint grimaced. "I am not sure if I would call this giving up. I just want my old wife back, my old feelings back. I want things back to how they were."

Matthew nodded. "I understand. I am here for you if you need to vent. It must suck to be the only unhappy brother when all of your other brothers have found love."

"That's very astute of you," Saint said dryly. "The first one to get married and the first one to divorce."

"Don't be morbid." Matthew frowned. "You are not divorcing. You are going through a rough patch, Sandrene will come to her sense, and you can sort this out soon."

Saint ran his fingers through his hair; he had a deep premonition that this was it for his marriage and the thought made him feel even worse than he was feeling before. He looked at the papers in Matthew's hands, to distract himself.

"What did you want to talk to me about?"

"Santa Maria Research Labs." Matthew placed the papers on his desk. "They were located in Port Maria, jointly funded by a Spanish pharmaceutical giant and our local giant Ryland Pharmaceuticals."

Saint nodded. "Why do you say 'were' located in Port Maria?"

"Because they are not there anymore. There was a fire in a section of the building." Matthew grimaced. "A gas explosion at the front of the building caused a fire that was quickly contained. It didn't spread much. They lost quite a bit of their physical research; no one was hurt in the explosion. It happened six months ago."

"So, how do we come into this? Sounds like an open and shut case." Saint asked.

"Well, that's what I thought too after Andy Ryland told me about it, but there is more."

"Andrew Ryland, Junior?" Saint grinned, "How is he these days? I remember before his father promoted him to vice president in the company we had to thoroughly investigate him even to what he was eating at night. Who does that? I still ponder."

"Andrew Ryland senior does that. The man doesn't trust anyone. Not his family or even the security we provide. We have to rotate his personal security on a regular basis. He makes us a lot of money, but it is a sad way to live."

"I agree." Saint nodded. "So why does Ryland Junior want our help?"

"Andy says he suspects that the fire was set deliberately. He says he can't get it out of his mind and he wants us to get to the bottom of it. The fire did not affect the back of the building where the storage area was, and he cannot account for six syringes of a drug called C3123, a memory inhibitor. He is suspecting corporate espionage. They were on Phase 2 of the trials, and the drug was exceeding expectations."

"What about the cameras?" Saint queried, "didn't they have cameras in the critical areas?"

"Yes, but they had a power outage an hour before the fire. It was while they were using their state-of-the-art new generator that it exploded. They lost security data for a few hours, and that is when their important drug disappeared. Ryland is thinking espionage. Many pharma companies are interested in the research."

"Sounds intriguing." Saint nodded. "Garland will salivate over this."

"He is finishing up a case." Matthew looked down at the papers on the desk. "I volunteered to do it personally, even told Andy I would get it done in two weeks."

"You?" Saint raised a brow, "field work?"

"Yup." Matthew nodded. "St. Mary is my parish, you know. The research center was just an hour's drive from where my uncle lives in Limestone Hill. I have been threatening to visit him at his country retreat in Limestone Hill for years now. He is due back from the UK next week. I could make it a mini-vacay while I poke around this case and give Andrew Junior some answers."

"Okay," Saint got up and stretched. "Go for it."

"Except I can't," Matthew frowned. "I have to go to the Montego Bay branch to sort out the surveillance system for one of our hotel clients. The head technician asked for my assistance. Computers are my specialty, not fieldwork."

Saint nodded. "I know."

"You are better at fieldwork. You've done it countless times and seemed to enjoy it. Besides, I checked with your secretary. You were going to take a month off, next month."

"For our annual vacation," Saint's eyes clouded over. "Kind of hard to do when Sandrene and I are on the outs, and she is working like a beast at the restaurant."

"Maybe you should still take some time off," Matthew said contemplatively. "You could fish in the morning, hike in the hills. There are places in Limestone Hill that appear untouched. It's even worse than where your uncle Micky lives. They have no phones, no technology. My uncle is the only one who has a satellite dish up there."

Saint massaged the back of his neck. "Sounds like a good way to escape but I don't know, Matt. I think staying here is the thing to do. I'll be putting twenty-four-hour guards on Sandrene, remember?"

"I know, but you'll get daily reports," Matthew shrugged, "once you go into the town, which you'd have to do if you are investigating the six missing C3123. Our St. Mary office has not seen your face since the grand opening last October. Brian would love to have you. He could even supply the manpower if you want it."

"I'll think about it," Saint said dismissively.

"Don't think too long," Matthew warned. "You have to start by next Monday. I promised Andy that I would get to the bottom of this in two weeks."

Chapter Eleven

"If you want to be fixed, you have to ask the maker to fix you." The preacher intoned. "If you try to do it yourself you are getting a bootleg job that won't last long!" He thumped the podium and looked in Sandrenes direction.

"Go to the source of life for your healing! Go to the great physician for your healing! Go to the Pathfinder if you need to find a way!"

Sandy looked down at her hands. Her nails were chipped, and her hand roughened, she played with a hangnail.

She very much wanted to chew it off, but the pastor was looking in her direction. She had the distinct impression that he was preaching at her. She was the only visitor at the small country church, and the preacher was happy to find a new face to unleash his sermon on because of that she couldn't get her nail, and she was obligated to stay awake and look interested.

It was hard though because she was tired and sleepy. Miss

Angie had her waking up at ungodly hours to go to the plot of land at the bottom of the hill and then to do a million and one chores around the house. It was never-ending.

She was bone tired and felt raggedy around the edges like she was a piece of cloth as if a small thread pulled would unravel her.

She wasn't meant for this kind of life. She could feel it. Call it a sixth sense or a deep abiding certainty, but she knew deep down that something about her life in Limestone Hill was off.

She theorized that Miss Angie was working her until she was too tired to think. She highly doubted that her past was the same as this, Miss Angie and Benjamin insisted that it was back in Westmoreland or May Pen or wherever they said she was from.

So how did they explain that her hands had not been as careworn or that she didn't have the same speech patterns as the market people around her, and she kept staring at food and thinking of ways to prepare them. Was she a chef in a past life?

Did she believe in stuff like past lives? She was not sure.

"You will be set free!" The preacher's voice was closer now, and she snapped her head up. He had left the pulpit and was advancing to the back where she was sitting.

"Will you give your soul to Jesus, sister? Will you be made free?"

He was speaking to her; there was no mistaking it. Sandrene swallowed. How did she know that she hadn't already given her soul to Jesus? These past couple of months were confusing, to say the least.

What she needed was to see a doctor about her condition, not a wild-eyed preacher who looked determined to add her to his flock.

She had contemplated walking into the doctor's office across from the market and throwing herself at their mercy, but Miss Angie watched her like a hawk.

They went to the market Mondays Wednesdays and Fridays, and she was not allowed to wander off by herself or to speak to anybody. Even the fellow market people kept their distance. They only spoke to Miss Angie and glanced at her furtively as if she had some type of disease.

Benjamin refused to answer her questions; sometimes his recollections of her past were in conflict. He couldn't keep his stories straight. One time her parents were killed in an accident, another time her mother died in childbirth, and she was made a ward of the state.

Sandrene was beginning to feel like a prisoner.

She glanced across at Miss Angie who was staring beatifically at the preacher as if he was saying something new.

The nightly meetings were supposed to go on for eight weeks. This was the first week, and the man sounded like he was using the same script night after night. He needed some fresh material, and he needed to read his Bible and understand it better, she thought.

Some of the stories he spewed from the pulpit had no resemblance to the ones that she read in the Bible when she went home to read them and confirm that she wasn't mistaken.

Benjamin shuffled his legs and glanced at her. He sensed her restlessness. He seemed to be in tuned to the confusion swirling in her and was sorry about it.

Sandrene reluctantly liked him. She didn't trust him, but she liked him. She sensed that he wasn't a bad person. Over the past number of months, she had warmed up to him gradually as a familiar stranger. Not as a husband.

Far from that.

She couldn't. If he touched her, even by accident she recoiled. He didn't pursue her sexually, and she was happy for that because if he made a move on her, she didn't know what she would do.

Lately, Miss Angie went on and on about grandchildren and doing her wifely duty with Benjamin but Sandrene was not having children with a stranger. Her mind was as blank as an empty sheet of paper, and she wasn't allowing Miss Angie to dictate her life. Not in that way.

Benjamin bless his heart seemed like he was patient enough to wait for her to get to know him better.

Tonight, he was in a blue and green checkered shirt and blue jeans, cleanly shaven and smelling like carbolic soap.

She probably smelled like it too. It was the only soap they had. It was slowly growing on her, the scent. Maybe that was how Benjamin would grow on her. He was a good-looking guy, in a clean-cut sort of way. He looked very familiar, but she was still searching for the spark that would have catapulted her into marrying him.

So far, she was coming up empty.

"The Lord wants you sister!"

She jumped guiltily because the preacher had drifted even nearer, and she had not heard a word.

"I am speaking to you, sister!" The preacher pointed at her. "You need to repent!"

What if I can't remember my sins? Sandrene thought frantically. What would I repent of?

She got up. Suddenly, the little church with its backless benches and its red polished concrete floors and the flickering lamplight seemed too claustrophobic.

The preacher looked taken aback when she jumped up suddenly. He opened his mouth in shock.

Sandrene walked out. They were close to the back anyway. She gulped in the mountain night air when she went outside and started toward home.

Home.

Somehow, the little house that was nestled two hills over did not feel like home. She would have to go downhill then uphill and downhill again to get to it. Limestone Hill district was hilly. The road was rocky in some places and pitch dark scary in others.

Miss Angie had the flashlight which had made their sojourn to the church much easier, but Sandrene did not care. She loved the solitude of walking alone at least for a while. It was easy to imagine herself just walking into the darkness and into a different reality.

She just wanted her memories back. She just wanted to remember her life before this place.

She walked as fast as her feet could carry her over the rough terrain, maybe if she walked fast, enough her memory would come back.

"Sandy wait!" Benjamin was behind her.

She continued walking.

"Please!" Benjamin had a flashlight, the light danced along the road as he came closer.

Sandrene stopped and glared at him in the dark. "Why can't I remember things? It's as if I just appeared here four months ago. I need to know what happened in my life. I am twenty-four years old! Or am I?

"I don't know anything. Is my name really Sandy? Who are my parents? It can't be true that I had nobody in this world besides from you and your mother. Are we really married?

"Did I love you? Do you love me? Somebody else must know me. Somebody else must be missing me. Who am I?"

She was screeching the questions to the night air. Benjamin

looked horrified and a little scared.

"Sandy, please. We took you to a doctor, and he said that you will eventually get back your memories."

Sandrene touched her head and swung to face Benjamin. "I went to a doctor?

"Yes," Benjamin nodded vigorously, "and I have been waiting for you to get back your memory. The doctor said we should wait. What's the use of me telling you things when you'll remember them eventually anyway. Besides, I might tell you the wrong things."

"Some of your explanations don't sound plausible." Sandrene grimaced. "It sounds like you were lying."

"I know." Benjamin sighed. "Some things I can only repeat what you told me, and I may not get everything right."

Sandrene still didn't trust his explanation, but she went along with it. He had never told her about visiting a doctor before.

"I don't want you walking alone along this stretch of road in the night." Benjamin fell into step beside her and shone the flashlight at their feet. "You might not believe this, but I care about you. I really do. I love you. I have since the moment I first saw you five years ago."

His voice cracked slightly.

Sandrene looked at him. She had the feeling that this was genuine information, genuine emotion.

It was a pity she didn't feel it, or else she could happily live on without her memory, but there was a certainty within her that everything was not as it seemed.

"Where did you see me?" She asked.

"We worked at the same restaurant." Benjamin sighed. "I was assisting the gardener, and you were...assisting in the kitchen."

"As a chef?" Sandrene breathed, "that explains why I am

always thinking up combinations of ingredients."

"And why Mama has you doing all the cooking." Benjamin grinned. "You do every dish better than her. You have a true talent for it. There was a herb and vegetable garden at the back of the restaurant, and you used to come around there and say, Benjamin, cooking is art and science rolled into one."

"You used to pick the tomatoes and the zucchini and the herbs and inhale them with the purest joy on your face. I...I miss that. You were so happy then."

"Where was this?" Sandrene asked earnestly.

Benjamin took so long to answer she was almost sure he wouldn't bother to tell her or tell her some half-baked truth.

"Kingston," he cleared his throat. "You lived in Kingston for a while."

"I knew it!" Sandrene stopped on the path. "Are my parents really dead?"

"Yes," Benjamin grimaced.

"Why did we get married? Where did I live?" Sandrene couldn't get the questions out fast enough. "Why did I move up here, it's so remote."

"You, ah," Benjamin closed his eyes, and the opened them. "We got married because I love you. You lived at an apartment in Kingston, and we moved up here because we are hiding from the law. Up here is perfect for that."

Sandrene gasped. "What?"

"I didn't want to say." Benjamin groaned. "Please Sandy, the less you ask, the better. In a way, your amnesia is a blessing."

"No, it's not." Sandrene felt a sense of dread creeping down her spine, "what did I do?"

"You stole something at the restaurant where you worked and you ah... had a reputation of sleeping with men for money."

"I what?" Sandrene opened her eyes wide. "I was a whore?"

"Unfortunately." Benjamin sighed. "But I loved you anyway. You didn't know better. You grew up rough."

She made that explanation marinate for a while and then she remembered that he said she was a thief.

"What did I steal?" Sandrene was appalled at herself. She couldn't believe it. Of all the possible explanations she wasn't expecting this.

"You stole jewelry from customers. Benjamin pushed his trembling hand in his pockets. He hated to lie to her like this, but this was his mother's brilliant plan to get Sandrene to fall in line.

"If you go back to Kingston you'll be put in jail for sure."

Sandrene was poleaxed. "I ahm, really?"

"Yes," Benjamin nodded. "That's why we keep you away from people especially when you go to the market. That's why we are so cautious, especially around strangers and you should be as well, okay?"

"Okay." Sandrene could barely squeeze out the response.

"What's my real name? I know you call me Sandy but is it short for Sandra, Santina, San-what?"

Benjamin sighed. "It's just Sandy. It's not short for anything."

"And what was my surname before Larson?" Sandrene looked at him fiercely. "Tell me."

"If I tell you and you tell somebody else you could go to jail for ten or fifteen years. Sandy Larson will just have to do for now."

Sandrene's heart started galloping in earnest. She had to take deep breaths. This explained everything.

It explained why miss Angie constantly asked her if she remembered anything, and why Benjamin lied to her about basic information. They were the good guys, and she had distrusted them.

"So, your preacher was right," Sandrene mumbled. "I need to repent."

"When you think about it, all of us need to repent of something," Benjamin said chuckling. "I don't think he can be wrong if he says that to anyone."

"So, did I give back the jewelry I stole?" Sandrene whispered.

"No, you sold them and used the money to pay your rent."

"I'm a criminal," Sandrene muttered. "A criminal who doesn't even remember her own name, who did some very, very bad things."

Benjamin stopped her and hugged her tight to him. "You made a mistake. That's why I am standing by you. You are not a hardened criminal, and you definitely don't deserve jail. Just keep out of other people's way, only trust Mama and I. Okay?"

Sandrene sniffed and hugged him back.

"Promise me, Sandy," Benjamin said forcefully. "I don't want us to get in trouble with the law for harboring a fugitive."

"I promise," Sandrene said in a puny lost voice. She shouldn't have asked about her past. It was horrible.

"When the time is right you and I can rediscover what we had and give Mama those grandchildren she has been harping on about."

Sandrene nodded in his chest. What else could she do, he was her savior. She was a criminal. The least she could do was view him in a more favorable light.

She had no right to be holding him at arm's length for so long. He must love her to be hiding her from the law and putting himself at risk.

"Okay." She said out loud.

"Come on, let's go." Benjamin kissed her on the forehead. "I am sorry to unload this on you tonight."

Sandrene did not respond. She was the one that asked.

She was still in mild shock. She was a criminal. Her real name was indeed Sandy. She wasn't even sure she wanted to know what her surname was now.

They walked in silence for the rest of the journey. Sandrene's mind was churning, and she barely registered when they reached home.

She headed to their bedroom, which had two single beds at each corner of the room. She turned on the home sweet home and headed for the poky little chest in the corner that contained all her clothes. She had only a few outfits and only two nightgowns—Miss Angie's castoffs, one was pink and one purple. They were billowy and huge and wouldn't be out of place in the nineteenth century. She changed into the purple one hurriedly.

Benjamin came in behind her and sat on his bed, she kneeled on the threadbare rug and closed her eyes and squeezed her hands together.

"God, please forgive me, I am a criminal, I have done terrible things. Maybe my memory loss is a blessing, and I have been so ungrateful demanding to know what lies behind the darkness. Please help me as only you can."

She didn't pray out loud. She never did. She got up and got under the stiff, scratchy sheets; they had been washed one too many times.

She closed her eyes and tried to imagine softer sheets in a comfortable bed, but all she could think of was the fact that jail was not better than this. She should count her blessings.

She heard Benjamin ruffling around in the bed beside her. She heard him blow out the light.

"You are not sleeping yet, are you?"

Sandrene opened her eyes. It was so dark she couldn't distinguish shapes in the blackness. It felt as if her eyes were closed.

"No, I am not out yet. I am sleepy though."

"It will all work out," Benjamin said softly. "Stop stressing about it. If they try to find you, we'll move."

"Thank you, Benjamin. Goodnight," Sandrene whispered. She closed her eyes and sighed.

Sometime in the early hours of the morning.

She had a dream. She was lying in a bed. The sheets were so soft and silky. There was a man lying next to her. His skin was like smooth caramel, curly brown hair fell over his forehead.

She stared at him and a smile formed at the corner of his lips.

"How do you know I am looking at you?" she whispered.

"Because I can feel it, your stare is like a caress." he opened his eyes, and she started to sing.

Green Eyes how could anybody deny you? Honey, you should know that I could never go on without you.

"Coldplay in bed." He grimaced. "That band follows me everywhere."

"Don't be a grump, Green Eyes. Your eyes are beautiful."

"And your eyes are the like hot sweet chocolate," he reached up to kiss her, and her skin trembled all over like it was being touched by a live wire.

"I love you," he whispered and punctuated it with kisses. "I love you now. I'll love you forever. I will never love anyone else."

"I love you more." She looked into eyes and pulled him down to her. "I'll always love you more Green Eyes."

"Never." He chuckled before he kissed her. It was a hot scorching kiss that had her jumping up out of the dream with her body reacting to the aftershocks.

Benjamin was snoring in the other bed. Her whole body felt hot as if she had a fever. She sat up in the bed breathing harshly like she had run uphill and could hardly breathe.

What a dream. She ran her fingers through her hair and then closed her eyes again. She wanted that dream back. It felt so real and was so vivid she wouldn't mind seeing how it would end.

But it didn't come back. She was awakened by Miss Angie's rough hand on her shoulder. "Time for work, gal."

Chapter Twelve

Saint sat at the back of the Waterfall restaurant on Tuesday evening with Garland. It was almost closing time, and the restaurant was busy as usual. It was near ten o'clock, and nobody seemed in a hurry to go anywhere. There was a private party in the VIP area and a birthday celebration that was winding down in the courtyard.

Garland knew the celebrant and had wrangled for himself a slice of triple chocolate cake.

He polished off the cake and looked at Saint with a sigh. "It's not a Chef Sandy kind of cake, but it can work."

"How do you know it's not?" Saint asked.

"Because your wife makes chocolate cake to die for. I can smell it from a mile away. And it feels like velvet on the tongue."

Saint chuckled. "Chef Sandy has a true fan in you."

Garland nodded and sighed. "Unfortunately, for the last couple of weeks she has not been in the kitchen, and Chef

Brown and the employees have taken to calling her Gangrene Sandrene."

"What?" Saint frowned.

"One person said she will blow up at the drop of a hat and they all feel as if their jobs are in peril."

"Goodness. I thought I was the only one seeing the changes." Saint folded his arms and looked at Garland. "Gangrene Sandrene sounds like an awful nickname."

Garland nodded. "I spoke to Sandrene today, asked her how she was doing et cetera. She was polite and distant, very much unlike the warm Sandrene who would greet me in the past. I must say though, watching her this past week has been uneventful. She goes to work at seven, has lunch by herself in the office at one, works until ten and then goes home to the apartment. Boring as usual but it might pick up on the weekend."

Saint nodded. "I hope not, boring is good news for me."

"She is pushing herself too hard." Garland grunted, "just watching what she does is tiring."

"I agree," Saint said, "She should hire somebody else to help out. She is doing the job of four people now."

"What about her parents?" Garland asked, "when are they coming back?"

"The end of the year. They left in January." Saint sighed. "I spoke to them yesterday. They are having a good time in Melbourne. They said they hear from Sandrene regularly and she is doing fine."

"Well, the restaurant is still open," Garland smirked. "Obviously she can manage quite fine on her own."

"What did you find out about Gracie?" Saint asked. "Where is she?"

"She is missing in action," Garland frowned, "fallen off the face of the earth. I mean, I don't know where she is. She hasn't used her credit cards or left any paper trail. She told you she was going on a cruise?"

"Yep." Saint murmured. "On a cruise with her current beau."

"Well, it wasn't with her last known boyfriend, Jose you said his name was?"

Saint nodded. "Yes, Gracie was with him in St Vincent for the last four months. They were thinking about marriage."

Garland chuckled. "Thinking about breaking up a marriage more like it. This Jose fellow is married, went back to his wife in February this year after a tumultuous time with Gracie. He said if he never heard from her again he would be happy."

"Gracie is such a liar," Saint murmured, "so where has she been this last couple of months while Sandrene takes up the slack for her? And where is she now if not on a cruise?"

"I'll keep checking," Garland murmured, "but Gracie obviously does not want to be found."

"That has never been a problem for you, finding those who don't want to be found," Saint murmured. "Find her. She disappeared soon after her parents left for Australia. Her absence is putting my wife under undue stress."

Garland nodded and got up. "I'll do that."

"Wait," Saint stopped him. "I won't be around for a week or so, but I want daily phone reports by phone."

"Sure thing boss."

Garland left.

The birthday party petered out, and the staff cleaned up around him. One staff member offered to tell Sandrene that he was there, and he waited alone in the courtyard when everybody left. He was going to have to work on this marriage.

Saint took a deep breath. One week without Sandrene had proved to be both a relief and a blessing.

A relief because he had stopped beating himself about his sudden waning interest in her sexually and a blessing because now he couldn't quite contain the yearning he felt for her.

When she walked into the courtyard and sat before him and smiled, he felt his heart melting. Whatever was wrong with him and whatever was wrong with her they could get through. He would chalk up the past seventeen weeks as a glitch.

"Hey," she smiled. "I am so glad this day is over."

"Hey," Saint smiled, "she looked tired around the eyes. I miss you."

She looked surprised at that.

"I miss you too." She sighed. "I was seriously thinking about us doing a do-over."

"Come here," Saint whispered. She got up hurriedly and came around to his side of the table and sat in his lap.

"You smell like chocolate," Saint buried his nose in her neck, but try as he might, the usual feeling of well-being that the felt when he nuzzled her neck in the past was missing.

He sighed. "I am sorry, Sandrene."

"Sorry for what?" She moaned moving her neck along his lips. "I should be the one apologizing. I said some awful things."

"Sorry for pushing you away. This whole thing has been my fault. I know I started it. I don't know how, but I lost my desire for you. I can't explain it."

While he was talking, he realized that he hadn't gotten it back. The spark wasn't there. That indefinable thing that he had only with her was gone. Maybe it had a five-year limit. He hugged her close to him willing it to come back. He closed his eyes and inhaled deeply.

He couldn't force it. The pure unadulterated sexual

attraction was inexplicably missing. They were in the courtyard; romantic music was playing in the background. There was candlelight and intimacy. Sandrene was in his arms, but he felt bereft, empty.

Obviously, he was the problem. It had been him all along.

"Hey, don't worry about it." she pulled away from him and stared at him concerned. "What's wrong, you look pained."

"I am not sure," he whispered. He touched her cheek, and she leaned into it. It was a gesture he was used to. In the past, it made him feel protective and wishing that he never had to let her go.

Today it was as if he was watching himself do it.

"You look so gorgeous," she whispered reverently. "I can't believe that you are mine."

Saint gave her a half smile. That was a very Sandrene like thing to say. It didn't spur him to say the same thing though, which he would have in the past because she did look gorgeous and he couldn't believe he had her.

But the declaration of her wanting to see other people, and the image of her sneering at him and calling him boring came to mind.

He inhaled deeply. He had deserved that. He had outright rejected her for sixteen weeks, rebuffed her when she wanted intimacy. Even now, while she sat on his lap, he wanted to push her away.

He was the one rejecting his wife.

"So how was your day?" She asked sweetly, too sweetly. It sounded fake sweet as if she were pretending.

They never pretended with each other in the past, except for the last couple of weeks and then he realized that maybe that was the crux of his rejection. He knew when she was less than honest with him.

"It was okay." He searched her face.

What was wrong with him? Why was he finding fault with everything she did?

This is Sandrene. The only woman he had ever loved. The woman he had thought he would love forever, and he still did, just not physically.

"My day was crazy busy. I have a million and one things to do, some of them are unnecessary. I think Chef Brown is out to get me. He never used to be this way with San...I mean my parents."

"Gracie should be helping you." Saint pointed out.

"Gracie is in adventure mode. She is in love and following her boyfriend all over the world."

"What's the name of her current boyfriend again?" Saint asked.

"Jose Santiago." She looked at him and raised an eyebrow. "Why?"

"Have you met Jose?" Saint asked.

"No. Why?"

"Because Gracie is not going out with Jose Santiago, they parted ways earlier this year," Saint sighed, "so she lied to you too."

"Why would Gracie lie to me?"

"Maybe because she always lies and maybe this new guy she is seeing is another married man?" Saint said disparagingly. "Your sister has the morals of an alley cat."

"Don't call her names!" Sandrene jumped up from his lap. "There is nothing wrong with Gracie's morals. She marches to her own beat. She does not view life the same way you do. It does not mean that she is a bad person. And why are you spying on Gracie?"

Saint watched, bewildered, as she readily jumped to Gracie's defense. "I apologize. I didn't say she was a bad person, but you can't deny, your sister is not the most discerning when it comes to men, nor is she responsible. She left you alone to single-handedly run this place. And you have to admit that it is stressing you out."

"I am running this place quite well by myself."

"The employees are calling you Gangrene Sandrene!"

Sandrene giggled. "It's terrible, but it does have a nice ring to it."

"No, it doesn't," Saint frowned. "You have changed. You would never want anybody calling you names. Your reputation is important to you."

He stood up too and narrowed his gaze at Sandrene, "Gracie said you went on a date last Monday, who was it with?"

"I didn't go on a date." Sandrene rubbed the back of her neck absently. "I went to the parents' house to pick up something."

"So, she lied again," Saint murmured, "and yet here you are defending her."

"Look, Saint, I don't want to argue."

"Me neither." Saint sighed. "Especially not about your sister. I do think you should get some help here though."

"I have interviews set up for next week. I already got the go-ahead from my parents. They have somebody in mind; he has worked here before and went away to study. He is practically a shoe-in if he says yes."

"So, I guess you forgot about our annual vacation," Saint asked and then ran his fingers through his hair leaving it tousled.

She took a step toward him and then another and touched his hair and smiled. "I like your hair like this."

"That's a first." Saint eyed her suspiciously. You always preferred it low.

"My tastes are changing."

Saint bit back an angry retort. It was going to be along the lines of, 'and so has your attitude', but he resisted.

"I am going away for two weeks. There is a case I need to check out. That leaves two weeks for us to go on a make or break vacation when I get back if you are interested. It should give you enough time to install a manager and maybe find your sister. That's if I don't find her first."

Sandrene cleared her throat. "Make or break vacation. I like the sound of that."

"I leave tomorrow." Saint pushed his hands in his pockets and rocked back on his heels. "I'll call you in the evenings when I can."

She didn't ask him where he was going; she didn't ask him why she would only hear from him when he could call; she didn't ask him any of the Sandrene like questions that he expected from her.

Sandrene did not like to be parted from him for long. At least the old Sandrene.

"You are not going to have your men watching me while you are gone, are you?" It was the question that clinched it for him.

The death toll on his marriage.

There was no concern, no begging him to take her with him.

"Of course." He looked at her and smiled coldly. "What are you planning to get up to in my absence?"

"Nothing." She shrugged and turned away from him, "nothing at all, not with you watching me."

Chapter Thirteen

Port Maria market was at a picturesque location beside the sea. The market itself needed serious updating but the area where Sandy sold cabbages, green peppers, tomatoes, and whatever ground provisions they had planted or picked from Limestone Hill, was not that bad.

They had a stall that Miss Angie rented for Wednesday and Fridays. On Mondays, they sold at the entrance of the market.

Getting to the market was a long, complicated maneuver that Miss Angie seemed to relish. Sandrene found it tedious and unnecessary.

Usually, they hired a cartman. There were two of them who operated in the district. These cartmen would take the produce to the foot of the hill in a twenty-minute journey where the market bus would pick them up promptly at six in the morning. There was a regular crowd of market women and men there. They all knew each other by name.

From there the bus would take them to Port Maria. It was an hour's journey from Limestone Hill.

At first, Sandrene was treated as the new girl, the green one, the novice, they had teased her that first morning and a couple ones after that when they heard her speak, one lady had said she sounded posh, but seventeen weeks later they were treating her like one of them.

Miss Angie was somewhat comfortable in allowing her to go to the market alone because she was ill, laid up in bed with a hot water bottle on her chest and struggling to breathe. She had asked Sandrene to take the five hundred pounds of cabbage to the market because she feared that they would spoil if they delayed in selling them.

Going to the market alone would have scared her normally, but Sandrene was too sleepy to feel scared. Besides, this was her opportunity to go somewhere other than the Port Maria market. She could go to a clothing store, visit a restaurant, look into a bank. Do something other than just the market.

As a prisoner to Miss Angie and Benjamin, she had no money for herself, and she had not been allowed to leave Miss Angie's watchful eye.

Miss Angie had pointed to the rickety dresser in the corner and hoarsely said, "Money for the bus fare, lunch and buy me some flu medication. Go to the pharmacy in the supermarket across the street. Don't wander around the town, Sandrene, and avoid the police station.

"If you hear anybody mention a restaurant or jewelry run," Miss Angie coughed and then wheezed. "Remember don't talk to strangers!"

That last bit had put a damper on her newfound freedom. She had forgotten that she was a criminal.

She had docilely picked up the tiny purse that Miss Angie had stuffed with money.

This was her get out of jail free card, at least for a little while. It was time to spread her wings, Miss Angie and Benjamin had her on a tight leash. Criminal or not, neither of them could oversee her today.

She had been chirpier than usual when she greeted John the cartman. Every other male in the hills was called John, there was John the electrician, John the shop man, John the preacher.

She had been grinning so wide that John had grinned with her. She never saw him smile and she understood why when he showed a row of gums and only three teeth in the bottom part of his mouth.

"Is a good day, Miss Sandrene." He said giving her a thumbs up. "I hope you sell all of these juicy cabbages today."

"Me too," Sandrene whispered, and she hoped that she sold them early.

The bus pulled up at six with much blowing of horn and fanfare. The conductor hopped off and helped her with the bags.

Sandrene entered the bus and greeted everyone. She sat beside Joy. She was a pleasant-faced woman who was much younger than she looked. Miss Angie had mentioned that she was in her twenties and Sandrene could not reconcile that age with the woman beside her. Joy seemed as if she had lived a hard life.

But she had recently found happiness with a man named Joe. All Joy spoke about these days was her wedding plans. She usually entertained the bus with what they were going to do next.

She lived in a place called Hillock, and it seemed like the whole village was contributing something to her grand reception.

"No Miss Angie today?" Joy asked when she sat down.

"She must be sick. Miss Angie never misses a market day."

"She is sick," Sandrene said. "Why else would she allow me out of prison and to be on my own?"

Joy looked her over. "You look different."

"New jeans," Sandrene pointed to the pants that Miss Angie had brought to her last week. They actually fit. She also got a new blouse, a very nice blouse that looked and felt expensive.

It was green with ruffles at the neck and sleeves. Miss Angie had handed them to her and told her she had bought them on sale.

"Yes, they fit," Joy murmured, "I didn't know Miss Angie had taste in clothes."

Sandrene laughed. "I had no idea either, but I accepted the clothes gladly. I had only a few pieces of baggy and ugly outfits that were the cast-offs of Miss Angie's daughter, Carlene."

Joy smiled. "Miss Angie should let you out on your own more often. You are pretty."

"Thanks, Joy."

"It's a pity you are married to Benjamin. You are too good for him."

Sandrene glanced at her sharply.

"Don't get offended," Joy whispered, "but we all know you are not one of us. You don't talk like us. You don't act like us, Miss Angie is trying hard to make you into somebody you are not. I can see that from a mile away. She keeps such a close eye on you that it makes me suspicious.

Sandrene inhaled. Joy's assessment was spot on. "I stand out that much?"

"Yes," Joy frowned, "and that stupid story about your memory being lost, I can't believe that."

"It's true though. I really can't remember anything."

Sandrene whispered back. "I can't remember my whole life before four months ago."

"You should go to the police then," Joy muttered. "Let them sort things out for you. It has been on my heart to tell you this. The Lord reveals these sorts of things to me."

"Thanks, Joy," Sandrene said grimly.

She couldn't go to the police. Surely, she would go to jail. She couldn't very well tell Joy that. She closed her eyes instead and murmured.

"Wake me up when we get to Port Maria."

"Sure." Joy said.

There was a slight pain behind her eyes from lack of sleep. Sandrene rested her head on the headrest and closed her eyes. The bus soon stopped for other people with market produce. She didn't open her eyes to see who it was.

She was having rough nights lately where she dreamed things, about disjointed events and situations. Her one constant dream though was that of a green-eyed man who she called Green Eyes. They were always in some intimate situation, and he always told her that he loved her.

Obviously, it couldn't be real. They were just fantasies. Men like him were movie characters. She was probably running through some movie that she had watched before she lost her memory.

Whatever it was, her fantasies were disturbing her sleep. Last night had been especially intense. The dream man had held her hand and told her not to forget him.

"Never forget me, Sandrene. Fight for us."

She had woken up with tears on her cheeks, her heart beating as if it were trying to race out of its cage.

She had sat up in the bed wondering what it all meant. She had no clue, and she wasn't going to discuss it with Miss Angie or Benjamin.

Even though she trusted Benjamin a bit more than she did Miss Angie she was still wary of bringing it up.

She hardly saw Benjamin anyway. He left before she woke up at four thirty and he returned home quite late.

He was working with the foreman at Blackwood Farms, Ted Nesbett, to clean up the property for Mr. Blackwood who was due to return home any day now.

****

"Is everything set for your St. Mary adventure?" Matthew asked when Saint entered the office.

"Yup." Saint looked up from his computer. "Just talked to Andrew Ryland Junior, he sent over a two-page brief about the drug, C3123. Apparently, it is very precious to his company, groundbreaking et cetera. He is in a panic over it being duplicated.

"He also sent over a list of the employees who were at the facility. It's not a long list, just ten employees. I already have intelligence running background checks on all of them including if there were any recent bank deposits made."

"I knew you would be the best man for the job." Matthew grinned. "I assured Ryland that you were the best and if anybody was going to get to the bottom of this, you would."

Saint nodded. "Well, don't praise me yet. I am feeling out of sorts today. I don't think I have my game face on."

"Sandrene?" Matthew quirked a brow. "Can I tell you that I am surprised by this turn of events. You and Sandrene seemed so perfect together."

Saint nodded.

"It's like we are in a weird alternate universe. "

Matthew sighed. "I spoke to my uncle, and he said he would love to have you at his countryside retreat for as long as you want to stay. He's returning to Jamaica today, here are the GPS coordinates to his place."

Matthew handed him his iPad.

Saint widened his eyes. "Matthew, this is pretty far from civilization."

"I know, but it is great. I wish I were going with you."

Saint drummed his fingers on the desk.

"Okay here is what I'll do. I'll stay at your uncle's for a couple of days and only because you insist but I am going to stay at GoldenEye Resorts. It's closer; it's just fifteen minutes from Port Maria, and the roads are better."

Matthew chuckled, "Not to mention it's in a gorgeous location. You get to swim every morning and night if you please and then there is the spa..."

"You sound envious." Saint chuckled.

"I am so envious I hear the theme song Goldeneye in my head." Matthew grinned. "I am so envious I am thinking of ditching this Mobay assignment and replacing you."

"Too late." Saint laughed. "You convinced me to take a break, and I am going to be out of here in fifteen minutes."

"And I am happy I did." Matthew grinned, "Try to have fun, man."

Saint nodded. "I'll try."

****

Trying to have fun was easier said than done. What he was trying to do was not to think about his failing marriage and that it was his fault. All this mess was his fault. He loved Sandrene, and yet he didn't.

What had started out as a great love story was now a nightmare.

His only solace was remembering the good times. And

that had been for most of their time together. He couldn't pinpoint any particular highlights that bested the rest. They were all good times.

If things were normal between them, she would be going with him on this assignment. They would be staying together at Goldeneye. They had stayed there for a week three years ago. He had booked the same beach cottage. He could picture her naked, lounging on the back porch with her feet in the water and a happy, contented smile on her face.

"Why can't we live here forever? Just like this."

"You want to spend the rest of your days naked in St. Mary?"

He had slipped into the water. "You'd get bored."

"I will never get bored with you," Sandrene had declared happily. "It's a good thing because we are forever. You are stuck with me."

He had loved to hear that because he couldn't think of anything better, being stuck with her as she put it.

And now fast forward a couple of years, she didn't even ask him where he was going, she just wanted to know if he was going to watch her.

It pained his heart to think about it.

He slammed the brakes on his thoughts and turned on the car radio to a sports channel. He listened to cricket all the way into Port Maria. He pulled up into the Wiley Supermarket parking lot. Wiley Securities was on the same building. The manager was expecting him.

He was rummaging in the back of the car when the hairs on the back of his neck stood on end. He felt a sense of awareness so strong that he actually paused and stepped back from the car.

And then he saw her.

She was walking by his car, totally oblivious that he was

there.

His heart started racing. He blinked twice. How on earth would Sandrene be in St. Mary was this some sort of surprise and why wasn't she acknowledging that he was there?

He closed the car door and followed sedately behind her into the supermarket.

Chapter Fourteen

Sandrene walked into the supermarket with an extra spring to her step. Joy had agreed to watch the stall and had encouraged her to stay away as long as she needed to. It was lunchtime, she was hungry, and she was finally free to roam Port Maria.

Joy said the supermarket had a café that sold the best foods and at a reasonable price. She headed for the sign that said Yum Yum it was off to the side of the supermarket and had its own entrance.

She had never been this excited about anything before. She happily approached the food counter, read the comprehensive menu and then ordered baked chicken. She had not had baked chicken since she woke up in Limestone Hill. Maybe she had it in Kingston?

Her eyes were drawn to it, and she felt a surge of eagerness when she ordered.

It was past lunchtime, and only a few people were sitting

in the café, so she was served quickly. She took her tray and sat at the corner of the café where she could see the people coming and going from the supermarket and the parking lot.

She would do some people watching while she ate, speculating about their lives and their loves, watching as they enjoyed their freedom.

She was probably grinning to herself when she sat down. She needed to stop, anyone observing her would think she was crazy, but being free did that to a person, made them giddy with it.

"May I join you?" A man stepped in front of her line of sight and then sat down before her.

She gasped out loud. It was him! The man from her dreams! Green Eyes!

He didn't wait for her to reply. He just sat and grinned at her. "You decided to join me, and here I thought that you didn't care."

She stared at him in fascination. "Who are you?"

He leaned forward. His green eyes seemed as if they were piercing through her. He ignored her question.

"When did you get here? Were you following me?"

"No." Sandrene shook her head in bewilderment. She looked down at her food, a feeling of panic gripping her.

Was this someone from her past? Were the dreams of him, a memory? Did he know that she was a criminal? Would he turn her in?

Her mind churned. She felt like getting up and running.

"Hey Sandrene, what's going on?" He whispered the question.

"I...I...don't know who you are." Her lips trembled. "My name is not Sandrene. She got up, "I have to go."

"You haven't eaten your food yet," He said pointing to her untouched plate. "I am sorry, for spooking you. Really, I am."

He stared at her wearily until she sat down again.

"This must be a case of mistaken identity," he murmured, but it was obvious he didn't believe what he was saying.

He was too watchful, too alert. He unfolded his arm and was staring at her fascinated.

"So, what is your name if you don't mind me asking?"

Sandrene's heart slammed against her ribs. He was even more handsome in person than her dreams. Who was he?

"Joy," she said the first name that came to mind. She was thankful that she didn't even know her own name.

"Joy," he repeated it and then nodded. "Okay."

"Who are you?" she whispered again hoarsely.

"My name is Saint Wiley," he looked at her, disbelief stamped on his face. "I am in security. Just came to visit my firm here in St. Mary and to pursue a case."

He was on to her! Sandrene took a sip of her drink and almost choked.

"A case?" She sputtered feeling cornered.

"Yep," he nodded. "Excuse me a moment."

He whipped out his phone and dialed a number. "Garland, where is my wife?"

Sandrene wondered if she should flee. She couldn't hear what the person on the other end of the line said, but Saint hung up the phone and then scratched his head.

"This is a pickle, Joy."

"What pickle?" Her voice trembled, jealousy scorched her insides. He was married?

And why should she care, she was married to Benjamin.

"I'll explain soon." He took up his phone again. "I just want to make sure."

He dialed a number and greeted the person on the other end.

The other person spoke to him. Sandrene strained her ears

to hear who it was but she could deduce from his end of the conversation that it was probably his wife.

"I know your day is busy, just checking in," he said calmly. "I hated how we ended things last evening. I am sorry I won't be around to sort things out."

He hung up after a brief conversation and then stared at her again. "Forgive me, I had a curiosity to sort out. You look and sound a lot like my wife and her sister. It is amazing when you think about it. If I didn't hear her on the phone just now and had her under twenty-four-hour surveillance, I'd think she was you."

He rubbed his eyes and then blinked rapidly. "I must be hallucinating."

"You have her under surveillance?" Sandrene whispered. "Why?"

"Because she needs it." He didn't elaborate as to why and Sandrene did not want to pry. She was curious though.

"You are from Kingston, aren't you?" She asked cautiously. When he allowed the silence to drag on for a while.

"Yes," he nodded, "You aren't eating."

He pointed at her untouched plate.

"I am not hungry anymore. Maybe I should take it to go."

"Go. Where?" He asked.

"I was working," Sandrene said reluctantly.

"Where?" he asked earnestly.

"I er..."

"I am not letting you out of my sight," he said forcefully. "This situation is too intriguing to let go, so you might as well tell me where you are going. I'll follow you all day if I have to."

Sandrene sighed. The one day she was on her own and enjoying her freedom she got caught.

She was going to jail. He worked in security! He was

having his own wife watched.

"Are you going to take me in to the police?"

He took a while to answer and then he shook his head. "No, but I'd love to know why you'd think I would do that."

Sandrene rubbed the back of her neck, and he followed her hand movements, a fascinated look in his eyes.

"I sell in the market. I have to get back."

He hid his expression well, but she could see that she had shocked him.

She had no time to assess why that would be an issue before he was leaning toward her again.

"Where are you living?" He breathed the question as if his voice wasn't quite steady.

"I can't tell you that," she got up. "I have to go."

She left the food behind. She hadn't even bought Miss Angie's medication. She hurriedly walked out of the building and glanced furtively behind her. He was staring after her, watching her walk away.

He wasn't following her, so she relaxed a little. Maybe he wasn't going to turn her over to the police, but he was acting quite strangely. Did she look that much like his wife? And what about her dreams of him?

It was him, no mistaking it, right down to his thick curly eyelashes.

What had they been to each other? Who was he?

****

Saint allowed her to walk away. His mind was churning up all sorts of scenarios. Sandrene and Gracie had a triplet. An identical triplet? A woman who clearly did not know him. There was no recognition in her face when he first accosted her. That was no acting. She was totally oblivious to who he was.

At first, he had thought it was Gracie, after all, she could not be found, but even Gracie was not this good an actress. And to add more mystery to the dilemma he had just spoken to Sandrene.

He drummed his fingers on the table. And then called Garland again.

"Hey boss," Garland said when he came on the phone.

"I just saw a woman, spoke to her, who looks just like Sandrene and Gracie but claims her name is Joy and she sells in the market right here in Port Maria."

Garland started laughing. "You can't be serious, boss. The parents didn't have triplets."

"I am serious, and no they didn't. Have you found Gracie? I need to know where she is but if she is missing in action why would she be selling in the market? Gracie hates rural living. She is a city girl through and through."

"I am on it, boss."

"In the meantime, I am getting to the bottom of this third sister mystery. Something tells me I am not going to like it."

He carried the uneaten meal to the counter asked them to make it to go, and then he headed to the Port Maria market, it was close enough almost across from the supermarket.

He glanced at his watch it was after two o'clock. She should be hungry; she had just left her food behind and looked at him fearfully.

And what about those questions about the police? What in the world was going on with this woman who looked so much like his wife, sounded like her, even felt like her. He had felt the chemistry between them as if it were a livewire. The chemistry that was missing between him and the wife that he left at home.

****

It didn't take him long to find her at the market. At least she was being truthful about that.

She was sitting in front of a stall piled high with cabbages. There were also cabbages behind her and beside her. The place was bustling with people. He waited until there was a lapse in customers at her stall before approaching.

"Hey," he said.

She jumped like a scalded cat.

"Your food." He handed the container to her. "You left it at the restaurant."

"Thank you." She took it from him reluctantly.

"I wondered how she ate so quickly, and she wanted to explore the town." The lady sitting beside her chuckled. "It was her day of freedom, but she came right back."

"Freedom?" Saint looked between the two women and raised an eyebrow.

"Her husband and mother-in-law have her under lock and key." The lady chuckled.

"Husband and mother-in-law?" Saint turned to Joy. "I am sorry if I curtailed your freedom. You look like my wife. I am still shaken by it, but I spoke to her on the phone, and I am intrigued by this."

The lady beside Joy got distracted with customers and wasn't listening anymore.

"I want to know more," Saint murmured, "is it possible that we can talk. Work out why you look so familiar? You could be my wife's long-lost family member."

She bit her lip. The gesture was so Sandrene-like, he inhaled sharply.

"I can't leave. I have to sell my goods." She looked beside him to a customer who picked up a cabbage. It seemed as if she did it in great relief.

She didn't want to interact with him, that much was clear,

and it peaked his curiosity even more.

"Look," he said when the customer left. "I'll buy all your cabbages."

"It's four hundred and fifty pounds worth," she breathed in shock. "What would you do with all of this cabbage?"

Saint shrugged, "I don't care, I need to talk to you and buying them will free up your time. What's the cost?"

She stammered out a reply.

He called Ramson the manager of the Wiley supermarket across the road. "Ramson, this is Saint, I have four hundred and fifty pounds of cabbages for you. Can you send someone to get them? I am at the Port Maria market."

"I'll send someone over right now," Ramson said unperturbed. "I heard you were going to be here for a few days. When are you coming over so that we can talk?"

"Later, I have an urgent matter to sort out." Saint reached for his wallet, pulled out the cash he had and gave it to Joy. "Here you are. Somebody is coming over to get it. Now the rest of your day is free."

"You ah, you just..." She looked at the cash and then at him. "I have to be on the six o'clock bus back to the hills. Usually, we take back about half of this."

"Now you got rid of it all. You made a good deal." Saint gave her a reassuring smile. She looked like a cornered cat, like any minute she would leap over the goods and make a run for it.

She stood up and looked at the lady beside her for help, but the lady was haggling over prices with a customer. She looked back at him with panic in her eyes.

"I don't know if this is a good idea."

"What? Buying all your goods?" Saint kept his expression calm and attitude nonchalant, but he was boiling with impatience. He needed answers, and he needed them now.

Two shop attendants from Wiley Supermarket headed toward him with trolleys.

"Mr. Saint Wiley," one of them grinned at him. He recognized the young man; he was the twin brother of one of his security guards, Ethan. That meant the smiling guy in the Wiley supermarket uniform was Evan.

"Hello Evan," He smiled.

Evan and his companion started packing the cabbage in the cart, and Saint raised an eyebrow at Joy.

"Coming? You can eat your lunch in peace. You did cut it short."

She paused for a long while. Indecision stamped across her face.

"Go." the lady beside her urged. "The man is an angel."

"Saint." Saint corrected her, "Saint Wiley."

"Even better than an angel, a saint." The lady grinned. "You don't feel like buying up all my goods, do you?"

Saint shook his head. "No, sorry."

Chapter Fifteen

"So here we are again," Saint sat down before her in Yum Yum and looked at his watch. "We have three hours until your bus gets here that's a lot of time to talk."

"I don't have much to tell." Sandrene tucked into her food. "I live in Limestone Hill with my husband and his mother, and they are simple farming people."

"Your overprotective husband and mother-in-law?" Saint quirked a brow. "Why are they overprotective?"

"I ah..." Sandrene bit her lip. She didn't want to blab too much of her story. She was still wary about this handsome guy who was watching her with such intensity it made her uncomfortable.

She couldn't quite believe that he was real. How on earth had she dreamed about him before she had seen him in person?

He waited for her to speak. He was a patient kind of person. Not overly excited or agitated, it had a calming effect on her.

He had a calming effect on her. When she looked at him, she felt safe. She relaxed slightly. If he were about to drag her off to the police, he would have done so by now, not pay for all of the cabbages. Miss Angie was going to be shocked that she sold them all.

"They are overprotective because I am gorgeous and there are a bunch of men who would try to take me away." She grinned. It was a joke.

But he didn't seem to get it. He looked at her solemnly. "You are gorgeous."

And this was coming from a man who could probably stop traffic. She smirked. "I was kidding."

"What's your husband's name?" He asked, probably sensing that she wouldn't be answering that question.

"Benjamin Larson," she said quickly. After all, Benjamin was not the one who was in trouble with the law, she was.

"I see. So, you are Joy Larson?" He asked the question, but he didn't need a response. He seemed as if he was repeating it to store it to memory.

"What is Limestone Hill like?"

"Lots of trees and hills. It's foggy in the mornings and pitch dark at nights."

"Sounds rustic," Saint murmured.

And somehow, he managed to make the word rustic sound seductive.

And suddenly she was more aware of him than she had been before. The word rustic conjured up an image from one of her dreams of him. They had been in a log cabin, naked. As all of her dreams of him seemed to be.

His eyes caught and held hers as if he knew what she was thinking.

"So, you sell at the market every day?" He asked. His voice was husky and rough.

It caused a tingling to start from her left leg and ran all the way to her hand. She stopped eating and clasped one hand in the other so that he couldn't see the tremor in them.

This was ridiculous. He was causing a sexual response by asking her a question. An inane perfectly innocent question. What was the question?

"I uh...what was the question again?" She asked out loud.

"Do you sell at the market every day?" He asked the question again and frowned. He could feel it too, the attraction between them. The heavy tension.

"Only on Wednesdays and Fridays. On the other days, I farm the land with Miss Angie, my mother-in-law."

He looked at her hands and then back at her face. "You don't look like any farmer that I know.

"How long have you lived here? How long have you been married? Do you have any siblings? What was your surname before Larson? "

He had abandoned the calm persona and was peppering her with questions.

"I've been here for a year," She said hoarsely, "I've been married for a year, no I was an only child, my surname before was Rivers."

 She made that last bit up and felt instantly guilty.

He rested back in the chair with a stunned look on his face and shook his head. "I can't believe this."

"What?" she asked curiously.

"You feel too familiar. We have this thing between us. Seeing you is like looking at my wife. I can't believe that you are Joy Rivers Larson from Limestone Hill. This is a mystery.

"Does the name Gracie ring a bell?" He asked the question almost desperately, "Sanya, Lamar?"

Sandrene cleared her throat. "Who are they?"

"People who will be shocked out of their wits when I tell them I met you here." Saint murmured.

"Where did you go to school?"

"Somewhere in Westmoreland." She looked down at her plate. She had no memory of school. She was only going off what Benjamin told her.

Saint brushed her cheek with his hand and then cupped her chin.

"Oh my goodness, Sands. This has to be you. I don't know what happened. I don't know what's the game at play here, but I could recognize you among a million people."

He used his thumb to play with the side of her cheek, and she leaned into the caress without thinking.

He pulled away his hand. It seemed as if time stood still.

She couldn't get her stupid brain to work but wasn't he a married man? Why was he saying stuff like that to her?

"Did we have an affair or something?" She asked slowly.

He looked at her and chuckled. "No."

"But you said you would recognize me anywhere, and you said you had a wife."

"I know." Saint nodded, "I am trying to reconcile the two thoughts. Because something is not right here. I want to meet your husband and your mother-in-law."

Sandrene's eyes clouded over. "I am not sure that is a good idea."

"And I am sure that it is." Saint's eyes roamed all over her. "I will have to change my accommodation plans tonight. I am staying at Limestone Hill instead."

"There are no hotels up there, silly." Sandrene chuckled. "When I say it is rural, I mean rural."

"I know." Saint shrugged. "I'll take you home tonight. I need to check in with my office. Will you promise me that you'll stay right here till I get back?"

"Sure." Sandrene nodded.

It was when he reluctantly left that she realized that he had called her Sands. That was close enough to Sandy. He was right. There was something confusing going on here.

****

Saint thought about leaving the woman who was calling herself Joy at the table. He feared that she would make a run for it, but he had to check in with Brian, and he had to have his office double check her claims.

He didn't understand the feelings coursing through him for this supposed stranger. The more time he spent with her, the surer he was that they were right together. He paused before he reached the office building and said a quick prayer. "God please work this out for me. I am confused."

Brian was in his office, on the phone. Their conversation was brief. Saint promised that he would come by tomorrow for a more formal visit, but he asked about Benjamin Larson before he left. Brian had never heard of him. He called head office and had the intelligence unit run through all the names that Joy had mentioned, hers, Benjamin Larson, Angella Larson.

"It is urgent," he said to his division manager. "Rush it through."

He didn't know how he resisted sprinting back to the Yum Yum Café. Instead, he walked as fast as his long strides could manage and breathed a sigh of relief when he saw that she was still sitting where he left her.

She had finished eating. Her lunch box closed, and she was looking around.

He sauntered into the area as if panic had not gripped him cruelly by the throat at the thought of her disappearing on him.

"Want us to go for a ride?" He asked when he entered the café again.

She got up. "Where are we going?"

"I don't know," Saint shrugged. "We'll see where the road takes us."

"I am curious about you," Saint said when they were on their way. He was driving along the coastline on the highway. Maybe they would end up at Strawberry Fields Together. The place was peaceful and had several coves and inlets. It would not be crowded at this time of the day, especially since it was the middle of the week. He drove in that direction.

He glanced at his passenger, and he felt the urge to stop the car and hug her and never let go. She felt that familiar.

"Me too." She smiled softly. "I mean I am curious about you too. Is your name just Saint?"

"Yes, it is." Saint glanced at her. He still couldn't believe that she had no idea who he was. There was some wicked game at play here; his mind and body were playing tricks on him.

"There is nothing much to tell about me. I have five brothers. I work in the security industry. We do everything from the high-tech stuff to investigations. I am here on business. There was a fire at a research facility in Port Maria, something went missing, and I am checking it out."

"And you are married?" she looked at him curiously, "are you happy?"

Saint took his time to answer. "I was happy for a long time but these past couple of months were pretty horrid. Everything changed. She changed. I changed. It's an ongoing bad situation. We decided to call it quits recently. How about you, are you happy with your husband?"

Sandrene looked at the passing scenery with interest. She

couldn't remember driving into St. Mary. "We ah, he is a good man."

"A good man," Saint repeated. "Are you happy with him?"

Sandrene frowned. "I don't know what happy is. I get up and I go to the farm. I go to church. I go to the market, I eat, I sleep. I get up and do it all again. It feels like prison."

She clapped her hand over her mouth dramatically. She had told him too much.

He pulled over the car and stopped at the side of the road. He looked at her intently.

"My wife would do the same gesture. It's uncanny how much alike you are to her."

"But you spoke to your wife today." Sandrene pointed out. "How could I be her?"

"Yes, I did speak to her." Saint heaved a sigh. "But like you, my days are a variation of the same theme. It does feel like prison but being with you makes me feel hopeful."

Sandrene nodded and looked at him wonderingly. "Yes, I feel the same."

****

They never made it to Strawberry Fields Together, what started as a drizzle became pouring rain in a matter of minutes. Saint had to stop at a picturesque spot by the sea and watch as the rain poured.

"It's the time of year for it." He turned off the car and stared at the woman who could be his wife.

Short curly hair, capping a perfectly shaped head, those lustrous brown eyes that could be sparking with anger one minute and lit up with laughter the next. Short straight nose. He had kissed the tip of her nose so many times. With her he had a nose fetish, well with her he had every kind of fetish.

Her nose lips, breasts, legs...

She ran her tongue over her lips.

She was nervous.

And so was he.

The tension in the car could be sliced by a knife.

This was tension he had not had with Sandrene for months. This was the missing link in his marriage that he was finding with a total stranger. A stranger who looked like his wife acted like his wife and sounded like his wife.

He forced himself not to pull her seat belt and then haul her over his lap and place his lips on hers.

She was somebody else's wife, for goodness sakes. What was he thinking here? He had come down hard on Sandrene for suggesting that they see other people, but here he was having vivid fantasies of kissing another man's wife. But he was feeling like he hadn't with Sandrene.

With this woman the chemistry sparking off both of them was enough to singe the air. He broke eye contact with her and turned up the AC.

She watched his hands as he fiddled with the car dial. He could feel her stare even when he turned his head away.

"Tell me, Saint," she whispered as he wrestled with his body to behave appropriately. "Have we been lovers?"

"Why'd you say that?" he whipped his head around and looked at her.

"I dreamed about you before we met today. Every night for the past couple of weeks and I call you Green Eyes."

Saint gawped at her. "Say what?"

"I saw your face in my sleep. We were er..." she cleared her throat, "mostly intimate in all the dreams. Did you know me from Kingston? Were you cheating on your wife with me?"

Saint cleared his throat. "I have never cheated on Sandrene. I love her. We were great until we were not. I can't explain this thing with you. You feel it too, don't you?"

She nodded. "I do. And it's funny, that your wife's name is Sandrene because my name is not Joy it is Sandy. Joy is the name of the lady who was selling beside me in the market today. I made up the surname Rivers. I have no clue what my old surname was."

She heaved a sigh. "I couldn't trust you with this info before because I... Anyway, I feel as if I can trust you."

Saint was staring at her transfixed.

"Can I trust you, Saint?"

"Yes," he said it in a shocked hiss. "Yes, yes, oh yes!"

"Benjamin said I fell and lost my memories, but before that, I was working at a restaurant and I...I... stole money, and the reason why I am here now is because I am wanted by the police."

Saint took minutes to process what she said. He was still as he tried to haul the pieces of what she said together and tried to make sense of it.

"He called you, Sandy?" Was the first thing he croaked.

Sandrene nodded.

"How long ago was this?" Saint asked.

"About eighteen weeks," Sandrene said hoarsely.

"That is when Sandrene changed." Saint hit the steering wheel. "That is when things started to go downhill in my marriage. Which means that the Sandrene that is posing as my wife at home is the one that I couldn't get myself to sleep with. I felt nothing for her. It felt like the beginning of the end of the marriage."

"But how could this be?" Sandrene murmured. "Do you think I am your wife?"

"I don't just think it, I know it." Saint husked. "I know it. I felt it the moment you passed me today. I don't know the details of how this happened but my God, Gracie has a lot to answer for."

"Who is Gracie?" Sandrene whispered.

"Your twin sister," Saint said. He removed his phone from his pocket and found the pictures. He had a big stash of them together.

She gasped when she saw the first one.

"Wow, that's my face."

"Let me show you something," he scrolled through until he found a picture of her and Gracie posing before the Waterfalls in identical dresses.

Sandrene gasped. "Oh my! I can't tell them apart. Which one is me?"

"That's your identical evil twin sister." He pointed to the girl on the left. "She is going to pay for this."

He wanted to push his nose in her neck and inhaled her deeply. He wanted to whisper I love you so, over and over again, but Sandrene was holding herself so tense and looking at him with a scared cornered animal kind of look that he restrained himself.

"What if I am not Sandrene? What if I am Gracie?" Sandrene asked fearfully. "I can't remember anything past the last four months. All I know is Limestone Hill and my dreams of you. "

Her lips trembled. "Suppose I am really Benjamin's wife, and all of this is a mad coincidence?"

"I am going to sort all of that out," Saint said grimly, "trust me on this. Obviously, you and your sister have identical DNA because I tested her when she was acting strangely. I thought she was you. I thought something had gone wrong."

Chapter Sixteen

Saint ran frustrated fingers through his hair. The rain had stopped, and he could see to continue driving.

Her questions were valid. The only evidence that he had to prove that she was Sandrene was his body's response to her.

He needed answers, and those answers were in Limestone Hill. He drove with one hand, all the while clutching her other hand in his.

The good news was she didn't seem to mind. She was clutching him back.

"Your husband told you that you've been married for a year?" He asked glancing at her.

She nodded.

"And that you worked in a restaurant? Did he say he worked there too?"

Sandrene nodded again.

"You were a chef, and you ran a restaurant called the Waterfalls. Has he ever mentioned it? "

"No. Benjamin was careful not to mention anything about my past. He said I would be better off not knowing. He did mention that I was a cook in a restaurant and he the gardener."

"The gardener?" Saint puckered his brow. "It would be interesting to find out if your so-called husband worked at the Waterfalls."

Saint's mind was racing. He stopped the car. He saw the beginnings of an explanation here.

He loathed putting her hand aside to make the call to Garland, but he had to.

He impatiently waited for Garland to answer the phone.

"Garland, find out quickly for me if there was an employee at the Waterfalls named Benjamin Larson. I am staying on the line."

Garland didn't take long. Wiley Securities was the security firm for the Waterfalls. They had installed a biometric fingerprint authentication system along with the regular ID for all the workers. It was useful for background checks since they were the ones tasked with vetting new hires. They had data on everyone that worked at the restaurant.

Saint glanced at Sandrene periodically and smiled like a sappy teenager who had just met a girl he had a crush on.

"Yes, there was a gardener here by that name," Garland said. "He listed his next of kin as Angella Larson. What's this about boss. Weren't those the two names that you asked intelligence to run through couple minutes ago?"

"Yes," Saint muttered. "You won't believe this when I tell you, but I'll keep you updated."

"Do you know anything about your mother-in-law?" Saint turned to Sandrene, "Anything at all would be helpful."

Sandrene frowned. "She is a hard worker, and very religious. She is okay when you get to know her, a bit abrupt sometimes. She is sick right now. She was struggling to breathe so she sent me to the market alone. I should be getting medication for her."

"I see." Saint frowned. The name Angella Larson did not sound strange to him. Where had he seen it before?

He reached into the back of the car, for his laptop and turned it on. He had the files for the Ryland investigation on his desktop. He pulled up the list of employees that he needed to interview. There was Larson, Angella at the very top of the list.

What were the odds that Benjamin Larson who worked at the Waterfalls, was related to Angella Larson who worked at the research lab? What were the chances that they were now husband and in-law to a woman who looked just like his wife?

He gritted his teeth. He needed more information before he jumped to conclusions, but he was itching to get to the bottom of this madness.

Just then it hit him; marriage records would prove if Benjamin Larson had actually gotten married as he claimed. He made one last phone call before he drove off. He needed to know if there were official marriage documents for Benjamin at the Registrar Department.

He called Garland who said he would check that out pronto.

Saint came off the phone to find her staring at him intently.

"I still can't believe this. All of this feels unreal. I wanted this… on some level, I always knew that Benjamin and Miss Angie were not being honest. And now that I have some answers. I don't know how to feel."

"It's understandable," Saint murmured, touching her cheek. "You know what is ironic. I came to St. Mary to escape the wife at home."

"My evil twin sister, Gracie?" Sandrene shook her head. "This is crazy! What kind of twin sister would do that?"

"The one who wants your life." Saint heaved a sigh. "We will get to the bottom of this. The thing is investigations like this take time, but I am motivated and if I have to throw all my available resources at this case, I will."

"I don't want you to spend another night with them if you don't have to and I don't want to be a kidnapper either. Just in case my wires are crossed, and this is just all one big misunderstanding, which I strongly doubt."

"I wish I could remember." Sandrene sighed, "This would not be an issue."

"I know," Saint said grimly. "Tell me what you can remember."

"Like what?" Sandrene asked.

"Everything, no matter how insignificant."

"Okay." Sandrene started talking. She told him about her waking up with a knot on her head, the worry that Benjamin had when he thought she was dead, her church adventures, the preacher telling her to repent, her dreams of him, and the last one where he said she should not give up on him.

"And I dreamed that after praying one night. I was frustrated with my lack of memory."

Saint glanced at her. They were almost in the town when she finished. Saint turned in at the supermarket. "You said you wanted to get something at the pharmacy?"

"Oh yes," Sandrene nodded, "Miss Angie's flu medication."

"I'll be here," Saint said huskily. "I have a couple more phone calls to make."

Sandrene exited the car, and Saint leaned back in the seat and closed his eyes. He had listened to her go on and on about her life in the last four months, and he had felt guiltier and guiltier after every word.

If she was Sandrene, he had failed to protect her though he was the security expert. The irony was not lost on him.

And what of her memory loss?

Total amnesia. What had caused that?

He picked up his laptop before calling Garland. He was connecting the dots, and he had a suspicion.

Surely it was not a coincidence that Angella Larson worked at the place where the memory inhibitors were stolen, around that same time his Sandrene at home started acting different and this Sandy lost all her memories, and Benjamin Larson resigned in May.

It was all too coincidental not to look suspect. He read through the file on C3123. The information was not too jargon heavy, but it did sound like something out of a science fiction novel.

Memories are formed through a connection of neurons which are supported by the protein, actin. Actin stabilizes your memories. When actin is disrupted, it can interfere with the memory web and how the brain reads these memories. In other words, if actin is disrupted, memories become unstable and scrambled. Creating a type of block that is as effective as putting a blackout curtain over a window.

C3123 is a memory inhibitor a brain curtain; it disrupts the connection of neurons which are supported by the protein, actin in your brain.

Disrupting actin can create numerous side effects, heart attack, stroke, coma and other effects previously studied in the laboratory.

However, our scientists have found a workaround to create a safe neural block. We have stabilized the effects of actin disruption.

We have created a drug that can quickly and safely shut down memories without many deleterious side effects, so far.

Still in the experimental stages, this drug is found to be

effective for as long as three months. One dose (6 mil cc) can effectively disrupt years of memories.

In one case study, we have successfully wiped away traumatic childhood memories from an adult over thirty. We have yet to finesse the drug for blocking selective memories.

He would bet his last dollar that Angela Larson was the one who stole the batch of C3123 from the lab and he was almost certain that Sandy was the recipient of the medication.

He had to back all of this up with facts though.

****

Sandrene got back in the car with two packets of flu medication. Saint was very pensive when she joined him. He had just hung up the phone.

It started to drizzle.

"Today is going to be one of those wet days." She made a face. "When it rains the house leaks. I hope Benjamin checked on Miss Angie."

"Benjamin Larson, twenty-five years old." Saint grimaced. "There is no record of him applying for or having a marriage license."

"You heard already?" Sandrene gasped.

"Yep." Saint nodded. "No marriage, no divorce, no criminal record. He paid his taxes. He had one formal job at the Waterfalls from which he resigned in May."

"So, I am not married to him?" Sandrene whispered a surge of happiness engulfing her. "I knew it. I didn't feel an ounce of chemistry. I kept questioning why I would marry him."

"No, you are not married to him," Saint said grimly.

"I thought you'd be happy about that." Sandrene chuckled. "This is proving your theory."

"It is, and I am happy about that," Saint touched her cheek, "but disturbed about others."

And then he sat staring through the windshield; she could hear his mind ticking over a mile a minute.

"I never slept with him or anything." Sandrene offered in the silence. "I'd tell him that it would be like sleeping with a stranger. He always agreed to wait until I got to know him. I think we would have eventually; I was beginning to like him. He was a pretty decent person, gentle, kind, considerate and..."

"Stop!" Saint looked at her fiercely. "I cannot listen to this, okay. He was your kidnapper, a criminal who deceived you. He does not deserve accolades. He lied to you to keep you in line, and he was playing the long game, waiting for you to trust him completely so that you would let your guard down."

"Don't yell at me," Sandrene growled. "I feel what I feel. This morning when I left the only place I knew as home, I thought I was a fugitive from the law and that my mother-in-law and very hard-working loving husband were finally trusting me with freedom. I need time to adjust. I still don't know you. Yes, there are pictures on your phone, but I may not even be your wife! I could be Gracie the other twin. Have you thought about that? You are not sure."

"I am sure," Saint said exasperatedly. "Your sister looks like you, tried to act like you but I never responded to her physically. That was the tell; she could trick my sight but not my libido.

"And by the way, these so-called good people that you are defending are nothing but two-bit criminals who drugged you with an experimental drug called C3123. That's why you can't remember anything. You didn't hit your head and had complete amnesia. They injected you with a drug that is in phase two of the experimental stage. There are three phases which means they haven't finished experimenting with the drug yet."

Sandrene looked at him bewildered. "I am confused."

"I know." Saint sighed. "Six of the syringes of drugs were stolen from the research lab where Angella Larson worked. I have no idea how much they pumped into you and if it will wear off anytime soon. As soon as we get to Kingston, I am taking you to the new lab so that they can monitor you because I want my wife back."

Sandrene nodded. "Okay."

She suddenly felt energy less like all the stuffing was knocked out of her. She felt equal parts relieved about what was happening and equal parts weepy.

"Maybe we should take our mind from all of this and think about something else," Saint said in the silence. "You left a stack of your Coldplay CDs here. Maybe some of the music will jog your memory, lift the memory curtains a bit."

Saint hit play on one of the CDs. He didn't look on which one.

When the song Talk came on, he groaned, this was one of them that she would bombard him with.

"I like this," She said after listening for a while. "Can you play it again?"

"Sure." Saint turned the volume a little bit higher. He would endure the song until the end of time if she wanted. "You loved this song."

"Yes." Sandrene nodded and started humming. Are you lost or incomplete? Do you feel like a puzzle, you can't find your missing piece?

She stopped and glanced at him. "Why do I know the words?"

"Years of driving me crazy with it. Singing it at the top of your voice." Saint grinned. "Even I know the words and trust me, I try not to."

They listened to the music. The dying notes, so you don't know where you're going, but you want to talk...nothing really making any sense at all let's talk...

Sandrene looked at him. "I have good taste in music."

Saint grinned. "I won't admit to anything. Your memory will come back, and you'll remember what I think about your choice in music."

"What do you like?" Sandrene asked. "What kind of music?"

"Contemporary gospel, C. Wiley is my favorite singer."

"A relative of yours?" Sandrene asked interestedly.

"Yes," Saint nodded, "my baby brother."

"You have other brothers?" Sandrene bit her lip when she saw Saint's expression. It was disbelief mixed with incredulity.

"Sorry, for being so nosy."

"You are not nosy, but this feels like I am just meeting you for the first time. You know, we have half a decade of memories together, and then this is like meeting you again. It feels strange."

"I know, imagine how I feel." Sandrene sighed. "Do you know if I'll get back my memories?"

"God, I hope so," Saint said feelingly.

"Because without them I am not Sandrene Wiley, your wife, am I?"

Saint looked at her contemplatively. "Not really."

"That's what the memory inhibitor is supposed to do, let you forget your life's events and then create a different you?" Sandrene looked through the window at the passing scenery, "make everything new and fresh again, like a rebirth. A mind makeover."

"You are still you." Saint murmured. "The drug might have messed with your memories but not your personality."

"Maybe my personality was shaped by my memories. The things I went through, my life events." Sandrene massaged her temples. "I will have to learn to be Sandrene again. Your Sandrene."

"That sounds like something my Sandrene would say." Saint squeezed her hand and released it. "I am not worried."

Chapter Seventeen

"**W**here've you been?" Carlene screeched as soon as they drove up to the yard in Limestone Hill.

"What's wrong?" Sandrene hurried out of the car in a panic.

"Mama is in the hospital. They took her there this morning. She was not breathing when Benjamin got home to check on her. He went to the market to find you to let you know, but Joy told him that you went away with a tall, green-eyed man, named Saint.

"Benjamin came back here and injected himself with something or the other. I found three syringes around him. He was passed out on the veranda. So, I had to beg Mr. Blackwood who just returned from England to help me sort out this madness."

Carlene growled. "You were supposed to be here. He is your husband. I have three children and no time for this kind of drama."

"How is Miss Angie?" Sandrene gasped. "And Benjamin?"

"Dying!" Carlene screamed. "You left my mother though you knew she was ill. And now you are back here with a man in a fancy car!"

She pointed to the car but couldn't see who was in it. The windows were tinted. "It's him, isn't it? The one you left the market with today. He is the one that drove my brother to inject himself with whatever. I didn't even know he did drugs."

" Is that fancy guy you went off with, is he the one who bought you the two suitcases of pretty clothes I found under Mama's bed?"

"What?" Sandrene gawped at her. "What clothes?"

"Don't bother with the innocent act." Carlene sneered. "There is a name for women like you."

"Mommy," Carlene's youngest child, came out of the house with a fistful of money. "What's this?"

Carlene gasped. Her eyes bulged out of her head comically. "Where'd you get that, baby?"

"Under gramma's bed. The little girl released the money, and it fell like confetti on the wooden floor."

Saint had been taking in the scene and listening as Carlene incriminated her mother and brother. He exited the car; he needed to secure the evidence. He had a feeling that his investigation into the whereabouts of the missing syringes, was solved.

And he had added proof that Miss Angie and Benjamin were paid to kidnap Sandrene. He stepped out of the car before Carlene could investigate the source of the bounty.

She swung back and looked at him and then stopped, her mouth open.

"Who are you?"

"My name is Saint Wiley, private investigator for Wiley Securities. I am going to ask you and your children to step out of the house while I collect some evidence."

"Investigator," Carlene babbled, "investigating what?"

"I have reason to believe that your mother removed property from the research lab at Port Maria. Where are the syringes that you found?"

"Over there." She pointed to three spent syringes on the veranda. "What was in it?"

Saint turned back to the car, slapped on some gloves and got some evidence bags. He always walked prepared.

"It's a drug called C3123. A memory blocker."

"My theory is that your brother and mother kidnapped my wife, Sandrene Wiley, gave her this drug to block her memory, fed her some stories to keep her quiet and complicit with them. When your brother discovered today that she had disappeared with a green-eyed man, me. He injected himself in an attempt to lose his memories of his wrongdoing. It sent him in a coma."

Carlene covered her mouth in shock.

"The money is most likely from a payoff. I am going to count it and then bag it. It is evidence."

He purposefully did not mention taking it to the police. He didn't know what he was going to do about all of this madness, especially if Gracie was behind it.

He took some pictures, picked up the bottles and bagged them.

"Saint," Sandrene asked hesitantly, "is there anything I can do?"

"No." Saint shook his head. "This should not take long and then we are out of here for good. I would take us back to Kingston tonight, but I need to interview Angella Larson about these syringes."

Carlene looked between him and Sandrene. "So... er... he is your husband?"

Sandrene nodded. "I think so. I don't know. I can't remember anything because of the drugs."

"I am going to need proof of this, Mister," Carlene said stoutly, Saint whipped out his phone from his pocket and opened the pictures app.

"Swipe to the right."

Carlene nodded. She ran through the photos and then silently handed the phone back to him. She paused at the one with Sandrene and Gracie.

"You have a twin." She looked over at Sandrene. "She looks just like you."

Sandrene shrugged. "Apparently I do."

"What are you going to do to my mother? Carlene asked pleadingly. "She is not a bad person, just a greedy one." She looked at the money guiltily and then back at Saint. "Have mercy on her, please."

Saint looked at Carlene fiercely. "For four months and a week, your mother and brother had my wife. Think about that. That's kidnapping."

Carlene swallowed. "This can't have been Benjamin's idea. He will listen to Mama, but he would never think up something like this by himself. I know my family; this has Mama written all over it. She worked at the lab; she stole the things. I don't know why they would have targeted your wife."

"I think I know." Saint sighed. "Show me where you got this money."

"Come Poochie," she called to her youngest daughter. "Show the gentleman where you saw the money."

Poochie was hiding behind Carlene's skirt.

She reluctantly let go and shyly showed them to the cramped bedroom space where a suitcase with the initials SW was sitting on one of the single beds, with clothes spilling out from the sides.

"Those were my things?" Sandrene asked incredulously.

"Yes." Saint took a picture of the room and then lifted the mattress. They found money in tied stacks under the bed. One of them had lost the paper that covered the stacks and had spilled under the bed. That was what the little girl had been playing with.

Saint took a picture, picked them up one by one and counted them, dropping them into the evidence bag. He had to go and get a bigger bag. He counted half a million dollars.

So that was the payment that was offered to them to kidnap his wife. Saint was steaming. He didn't know how much longer he could pretend to be calm and detached.

He was fuming at himself, at Gracie who he strongly suspected was behind this and Miss Angie and Benjamin who had played doctor with Sandrene's life.

Sandrene docilely followed him to the car. She was not as angry at the two people who duped her and made her live a life that was not hers because she could not remember what life was like before.

It was going to be an uphill battle to get her well again. What if she never regained the memories that the drug suppressed? Would she ever be the same again?

He grimly started the car; he had to give Andrew Ryland a call about this. Maybe there was an anecdote?

"Where are we going?" Sandrene asked in a low voice. They had found two suitcases with her initials on them. They were filled with clothes and toiletries. Some of them he recognized. She clutched one now, a slinky tiger print summer dress. She looked like a little girl who was lost.

"My office in Port Maria. I'll have them store the evidence, and then I'll take you to the hotel that I booked so that you can have a good night's sleep. You can start putting all this behind you, Sandrene."

She nodded doubtfully. "What about Benjamin and Miss Angie? How are we going to know if they are okay?"

"You still care about them, don't you?"

"Well, they are all I know," She said helplessly. "I can't just turn off the concern."

Saint nodded. "I understand."

"I'd like to know what happened to them."

"Yes," Saint said through gritted teeth. "I'll make a stop by the hospital, and then we'll find out."

"Thank you." Sandrene settled back in her seat. She closed her eyes, a tired frown between her brow. He wanted to smooth it out and tell her she had nothing to worry about. He wanted to tell her that he had this. But did he?

What if Sandrene didn't want them to be a couple anymore?

He had been so busy getting to the bottom of things that he had not realized that this could be the end of his marriage.

He was a stranger to her.

A stranger to his own wife.

****

They arrived at the hospital a little after seven. Saint spoke to a friendly nurse who took them to a semi-private room. Mr. Blackwood was her benefactor. The nurse mentioned how lucky Miss Angie was to have him looking out for her.

She flirted with Saint all the way to the ward, completely ignoring Sandrene.

There were two persons in the room, separated by a curtain. Miss Angie was hooked up to a drip.

"Pneumonia," The nurse said looking at her medical file. "She is still not out of the woods yet. If she had not reached here when she did, she would be a dead woman."

Sandrene looked down at Miss Angie sorrowfully. Her larger than life personality was not evident. She looked frail and small. Her breathing sounded painful. How had she deteriorated so fast? When she had seen her in the morning, she had not been so ill. As far as she knew, Miss Angie had just had the flu.

She picked up Miss Angie's hand in hers and patted it. "I am sorry, Miss Angie."

Miss Angie opened her eyes slowly. "Sandy. Did you sell any of the cabbage?"

"She sold them all." Saint walked up to the bed. "Mrs. Larson, did you steal six syringes of the drug C3123 from the Port Maria Research Lab?"

Miss Angie opened her eyes wider. "Who are you?"

"Sandrene's husband." Saint was not mincing words; his stare was cold and frosty.

"Yes, I did." She closed her eyes. "I gave two to Gracie, and I kept four. It was only supposed to make her forget for a while. She paid me for it."

"Who paid you?" Saint asked. "Did Gracie pay you?"

Miss Angie inhaled and then exhaled, her breath rattled in her chest. She didn't answer his question. "I injected Sandy with one from my stash."

"That would make three injections in four months." Saint gritted his teeth. "Were you trying to kill her?"

"No." Miss Angie looked up at him, her eyes wet. "I am sorry," she gasped painfully, "Benjamin did not want to do this, but I convinced him..."

"Benjamin is in a coma," Saint hissed. "He injected himself with all three of your remaining stash this evening."

Miss Angie's chest heaved up and down, and tears flowed freely from her eyes. "I am sorry."

Her breathing became shallower and noisier as if she was

gasping for breath.

Saint stood there and looked down at her. Sandrene was the one who panicked and ran to get a nurse.

"She is getting worse," she heard one nurse say to another. "We have to page the doctor."

"I hope nobody mentions to her that her son is dead. Whatever it is that he had taken gave him three massive heart attacks in quick succession."

"Such a tragedy." The other nurse muttered. "A tragedy."

Sandrene stilled in horror. Benjamin was dead?

The tears were gathering to fall. Her eyes met Saint's he had overheard the nurses as well.

"Come here," he said huskily.

She walked into his arms and started to cry. She didn't know why she wept. By all intents and purposes, Benjamin and Miss Angie were not the best people, but they had been familiar.

She also cried for herself. She felt lost and afraid. She clutched Saint's shirtfront and would not let him go.

Chapter Eighteen

Messy. The whole situation was messy. Saint paced the deck of the beach house. The deck extended out to the sea. He had tried to tire himself with a midnight swim, but that was not happening. He was more alert than ever.

He stopped pacing and sat down at the edge of the deck with his foot in the water. If there was one thing that could sell Goldeneye, besides the beauty of the place with its lush gardens and warm Caribbean Sea just outside his doorstep, it was the peace.

The gentle lap of the water should have soothed his feverish brain by now, but it hadn't.

Sandrene had taken an early night and was curled up in the guest room in her boy shorts and t-shirt. She had told him a woebegone goodnight after they ate. The dinner was good. He had tried to be upbeat company, but the more he talked, the more she had retreated into her shell until she had told him that she was sleepy and then left for to the guest room.

He glanced at his watch. It was a little past twelve. He picked up his phone and debated which brother to call. Not Guy, he was on his honeymoon. Not Preston he had a newborn who messed with his sleep, not Jordan he was probably beat from his job on the construction site, not Walter, he was usually grumpy after twelve, not Case he was probably just getting back from a show.

He was feeling lost. He didn't know that he ever would be the brother who felt lost who had wife problems. His problems were huge. The brothers usually trashed out their problems together. At least he had a support group who he could dump his problems on. Not tonight though.

He put the phone down and sighed. He didn't want to disturb them. He jumped when the phone vibrated.

It was Walter's number.

"Hey," he answered in relief, "I wanted to talk to somebody, but I wasn't sure which one of you would be up."

"I am," Walter said, "I called you today, your phone was busy. You weren't answering, and then I realized that I didn't know where you were."

"GoldenEye." Saint sighed.

"You took your vacation and didn't say anything to me." Walter sounded wounded. "I had to ask your friend Matthew where you were. Even Preston didn't know where you were and you two are neighbors."

"Sorry about not checking in." Saint grinned even though Walter couldn't see him. Walter was sounding a bit like Preston and Jordan, mother hen's no matter how old he was.

"You should be sorry. I couldn't go to bed not knowing if you were dead or alive."

"I am alive." Saint sighed. "And I have a whopper of a story to tell you."

"What is it?" Walter asked.

"You won't believe it." Saint dragged out the suspense.

"Are you going to tell me tonight?" Walter asked grumpily.

"Maybe I shouldn't, you won't be able to sleep." Saint teased. "You'll never guess what it is."

"Okay I'll bite," Walter said grumpily, "you and Sandrene are back together ensconced in the beauty of GoldenEye you rediscovered your love."

"We are together," Saint snorted, "but only because I came to St. Mary to solve a case…she passed me heading into the supermarket. She did not recognize me."

"What are you talking about?" Walter asked. "You shaved your head and dyed yourself blue?"

"No," Saint chuckled. "She did not recognize me because she doesn't have any memory of us. The Sandrene that I have been living with for the past four months has been a knockoff. Fake."

"I have to sit." Walter whistled. "Tell me more."

When Saint finished, ending with Benjamin Larson's death, Walter was quiet.

"Oh, my goodness," He finally said.

"I know." Saint sighed, "and the bad part about all of this is that she is grieving over this man. You should have seen how heartbroken she was all night. I saved her from him and his mother, and she is looking at me as if I am a stranger."

"Are you sure that she is Sandrene and not Gracie?" Walter asked doubtfully. "Are you absolutely sure?"

"Yes." Saint sighed. "This is my wife. She feels right. I desire her. I love her. For the past couple of weeks, I haven't felt a thing for the fake Sandrene at home."

"And now you desire the one you found?" Walter asked incredulously. "Didn't you tell me that you did a DNA test on Sandrene?"

"Yes." Saint sighed. "They are identical twins they

probably have the same DNA. I would need to get a more in-depth DNA analysis to determine otherwise."

"You are right, this is a brain twister," Walter murmured. "So, Gracie lived with you both for months, so she could research a way to pull this off, didn't she?"

"I don't know." Saint sighed. "She was obviously up to something."

"Did she say anything to tip you off?" Walter urged.

"Yes!" Saint gritted his teeth, "every day. I thought Sandrene changed. Everybody thought Sandrene was acting weird. They were calling her Gangrene Sandrene at work."

"It was a genius plan on Gracie's part." Walter sounded like he still couldn't believe it. "She studied her sister and then tried to take over her life. Except she didn't bank on you having a discriminatory penis."

Saint chuckled dryly. "Discriminatory is right."

"I wonder if Aisha had a twin sister who looks exactly like her and acted like her to a point if I would be just as discriminatory? Or would I just blissfully live my life without a thought that I had an imitation wife."

"I think you should be thankful that Aisha does not have an evil identical twin."

"Yes I am, but it's fascinating. What if I had a twin brother who took my place? Would Aisha be discriminatory, or would she just have sex with him and have his babies and then when they find me the real husband, she wouldn't want to be with me anymore?"

"Don't get carried away, Walter." Saint inhaled raggedly.

"Did Sandrene have sex with her new husband?" Walter asked cautiously. "What if she is pregnant right now? Would you step in as a father?"

"No, she didn't and yes I would." Saint massaged the back of his neck. "She will always be the love of my life.

She didn't have any reason to believe that the life she was living was a hoax, it would not have been her fault. It would devastate me, but I would survive."

"You see why we were appalled when you were going to get a divorce," Walter said a smile in his voice. "So, when are you going to confront Gracie, let her rot in prison for kidnapping, stolen property, murder…"

"There is no murder. Benjamin injected himself deliberately, maybe he wanted to forget what he had done." Saint sighed. "I can't imagine why he did that. Andrew says the drug inhibits protein or something of the sort. Too much at once made his heart muscle explode like a balloon."

"Grim," Walter murmured, "There is a lesson in not playing doctor with medications."

"Especially experimental ones," Saint exhaled tremulously. "That could have been Sandrene. The idiots could have injected her with the drug and killed her."

"But it didn't," Walter said quickly. "Don't dwell on that what if. Is the chemical amnesia reversible?"

"Yes." Saint ran his fingers through his hair and started pacing again. "I spoke to Andrew Ryland tonight, told him about the situation. He said they were working on an experimental antidote called C3124. It is very experimental. And I really don't want Sandrene to take any more drugs that could harm her, so the only option is to wait. Tomorrow I'll check her into the new lab."

****

Gracie was sitting at her desk, looking over the wine list for the week when Chef Brown walked into the office and sat before being invited.

"What is it?" She growled.

She hated his insubordination. He ignored her and did what he wanted anyway.

"I heard that a past employee of ours died, Benjamin Larson. Back when you were a nice person and not Gangrene Sandrene, you had liked him. You told me that he had potential and was a good person."

Gracie gasped. "What? Benjamin? How?"

"Apparently he injected himself with some drug or the other." Chef Brown sighed, "It caused his heart to explode."

"Drug? What kind of drug?" Gracie was shell-shocked. What would it mean for the plan? She needed him for the plan to be successful.

"How did you find out about this?"

"I was the one who got him the job here, remember?" Chef Brown sneered. "I told you that I knew this young man from my mother's community in Limestone Hill who could do the job?"

"Yes, yes," Gracie said absently.

"You seem to forget a lot of things these days, Sandrene." Chef Brown shook his head. "I must say that I am disappointed in your attitude. You act more like Two-Face Sandrea Grace."

He was really into nicknames, the pig. She strongly resisted the urge to call him Fat Clown Chef Brown, but she had other things to think about than Chef Brown's stupid nicknames and his blatant disapproval of her.

She didn't know what he was whining about. She stayed out of his way most of the time. How was she acting differently than Sandrene?

"So er, how is Benjamin's mother taking this?" She cleared her throat. "I should give her a call."

Chef Brown opened his mouth and then closed it. "Sometimes I see a glimmer of the woman you used to be and then at other times I am baffled."

Gracie drummed her fingers on the table. Now she was sure to be in trouble. Where was her sister in all of this? Had she gotten back her memory? Had she figured out anything?

"I really should give Miss Angie a call."

"It won't do any good; she is in the hospital with pneumonia. I doubt she can answer her phone. My sister said something strange to me though, said Benjamin had a wife. I had no clue that he had gotten married. He was always so interested in you, but crushes crash, don't they? Maybe if you called Miss Angie's phone, you would get the wife."

He got up. "Glad to see some glimmer of the girl you used to be."

Gracie gave him an insincere smile and waited until he left the office. She grabbed her phone and punched in Benjamin's numbers. Chef Brown was messing with her it could not be true.

"Benjamin's phone." A teary voiced answered.

"Who is this?" Gracie hissed.

"Carlene, his sister." There was a sob and then a sniff.

"Is he really dead?" Gracie asked a sliver of fear ran down her spine.

"Yes." Carlene sniffed. "Yes. I don't know anything about funeral arrangements or anything right now. It just happened last night."

"That's okay," Gracie said huskily, "Do you know where his wife is?"

"She wasn't his wife. She was married to some other dude. He left with her last night."

"Was his name Saint Wiley?" Gracie asked really slowly and really carefully.

"Oh yes, that's the name," Carlene said, "I have to go."

She hung up. Gracie slowly put the cell phone down and

then stood up. Her legs were shaking. She was in trouble.

She knew Saint Wiley. By now he had probably uncovered the plan and was on his way to confront her. He probably would have a cadre of police and soldiers with him when he came.

Sandrene would win.

Gracie sat back down with a thump. Where could she go? She had dipped into Sandrene's account and paid Miss Angie and Benjamin. She had also transferred a considerable sum into hers.

Her sister's personal account was loaded. She had not dared touch the joint account Sandrene had with Saint, she had a feeling if she did she would be questioned about it and her cover would be blown but now it wouldn't matter would it?

She needed to go somewhere that did not have an extradition treaty with Jamaica. Where was that? She had no clue. She never needed to know and did think she needed to plan that far ahead.

She got up and started pacing restlessly. Jason was a lawyer, wasn't he? Her loyal lap dog. He would do anything for her. He would help her.

She dialed his number.

Chapter Nineteen

Sandrene snuggled in the sheets with her eyes closed. The sheets were smooth and soft and smelled perfumy. She was obviously dreaming. She could hear the sea. It was so near. She shifted in bed and touched an arm. It was her dream again. It was him. Her dream lover.

She didn't want to wake up like all the other times. She ran her hands over his back. He felt so firm, so real.

She could feel him turning.

"Hey," he said huskily.

"Hey, Green Eyes." She murmured.

"Are you still sleeping?" His breath fanned her cheek.

"No, I think I am awake."

"Did you dream about this?" Saint murmured. He let his tongue dart between her parted lips, and she involuntarily moaned, it was like coming home. She ran her hands through his hair, it felt like fine silk.

He deepened the kiss, and her whole body felt electrified.

Just one kiss, just one kiss, she promised herself, like an alcoholic craving what she knew she shouldn't have.

This was a dream, wasn't it? It was familiar. It was the kiss that woke her up at nights, the touch that made her fall apart.

"Do you want us to do this before you get your memory back?" he murmured in her ear.

"Yes." She whispered her body was on fire.

"Open your eyes." He shifted his weight, and her eyes flew open.

He was still there. This was no dream.

"Hey," Saint smiled. His curls were ruffled, his eyes were limpid. His body rippled with muscles as he moved.

"This is real?" Sandrene asked breathlessly.

"Yes." Saint nodded.

"Where are we?"

"Goldeneye," Saint whispered. "The resort. We've spent a week here together before. You said this was your favorite place in the world and that you would much rather stay here completely naked."

"I did?" She got up shyly her legs shaking. She pulled down her t-shirt, which had ridden up, to her breasts.

Her aching breasts.

She wanted to go back into the bed and finished what they started, but she needed to make sure that she was who he said she was and that she had a verifiable identity.

He laid back down in the bed. Looking impossibly inviting. "I am yours you know that. All of me is yours."

"But we are not sure who I am. I am not sure. And until I am sure, I won't..." Sandrene bit her lip. "Only when I am sure."

"Okay." Saint ran his fingers through his hair ruffling it further. "I can be patient. I have been patient."

"Thank you," she heaved a sigh and headed to the bathroom.

But she wasn't so confident that she could be patient, her body knew him. Her mind didn't, but her body did.

The drive into Kingston was solemn. Saint spent most of his time on the phone. She spent the time acquainting herself with the scenario and listening to her favorite music. She liked every song played and found herself singing to them. Like she knew the words and the music, and she knew what was coming next on the album.

Saint was between calls when he commented. "It's amazing, Coldplay survived your amnesia."

Sandrene giggled. "And you too, Green Eyes."

The song Green Eyes was playing, and she turned it up. "I don't know, but I think this is my favorite song of all of them."

Saint looked at her as she belted out the song. Rocking in her seat like old times, she didn't know how familiar it looked. They had done the same thing a thousand times, and he had indulgently watched her. Much like what he was doing now.

"So where are we going?" she glanced at him mid-song.

"To the research center. And then home. My brothers and their wives are all anxious to see you."

"So, when are we going to see Gracie?" Sandrene turned down the music and glanced at him.

"After we go home." Saint sighed. He had not made up his mind what to do about Gracie.

She deserved punishment. This stunt was beyond terrible. His brothers were all ready to lynch her and hang her at high noon. Walter had spread the news and one by one they had all called wanting more details. And all of them thought that Gracie should be in jail now.

****

The research center was relocated to downtown Kingston in the business district. When they arrived, Andrew Ryland himself greeted them. He was very apologetic. As if he wasn't as much of a victim as they were.

Four doctors looked over Sandrene and gave her a battery of tests.

Saint waited in the head doctor's office with Andrew.

"When will she get her memory back?" Saint asked when he sat down.

"We have to wait for Dr. Peters. He is in charge of the project." Andrew sighed. "Benjamin Larson unwittingly pointed out a side effect in the medication. 18 ml of it will kill a relatively young person who doesn't smoke or drink."

Saint nodded. "That's right."

"I called the hospital this morning," Andrew said, "I am personal friends with the administrator."

"And I heard that Angella Larson is getting better. She doesn't know about Benjamin just yet."

"Will you press charges?" Saint said, "I have the evidence."

"I think losing her son is punishment enough. I am just happy this was not espionage. I can sleep better tonight." Andrew smiled. "The question is, will you report this to the police. They kidnapped your wife."

"As you said, losing Benjamin was punishment enough. I think I am going to go after the brains behind this operation," Saint murmured.

"The sister?" Andrew whistled. "Family? What was her motivation? She wanted to be with you?"

"I don't know." Saint shrugged. "Maybe she wanted to be her sister, live her life."

"Either way this was sick. What did the parents say?"

"They will be here day after tomorrow. They are appalled."

Andrew took a phone call and shortly after did Saint as

well.

It was Garland. He had been watching Gracie.

"She saw a lawyer last night. Jason Lynch, you know him?" Garland asked.

"Met him once," Saint said, "She strings him along, treats him like dirt, and he seems to love it."

"Well, they had a power meeting for almost three hours," Garland grunted. "She woke up early this morning and had a meeting with him again. She is now in the office."

"Thanks, Garland. We need a power meeting of our own when Max gets back at the end of the week."

"Yes, boss. I can't wait for you to make this right."

Neither could Saint.

Before they could leave, the doctors had to know when she got the injections in order to ascertain when it would wear off.

Andrew spoke to his friend at the hospital who spoke to Angella Larson who gave them three dates. May 2nd, May 15th, and May 30th.

Barely two weeks apart. The last dosage had sent Sandrene in a coma.

Saint could have lost her, and he probably would not have known about it.

The doctors concluded that none of her internal organs were damaged, but they would like to monitor her weekly.

Sandrene was silent on their way home. She had turned off the music when they started the car.

"I could have died. Like Benjamin," She whispered.

"I know." Saint took her hand and squeezed it in his.

"My own sister did this?"

Saint nodded. "Yes, she did."

"Was I mean to her?" Sandrene whispered. "I don't understand."

"You don't have a mean bone in your body," Saint reassured her. "Don't stress yourself about this. Gracie did all of this because she has always had a chip on her shoulder where you are concerned."

He changed the subject. "My brothers are extremely excited to see you. I told them not to stop by today, but I am afraid there is no stopping them."

****

It was in the late evening when Saint opened the door to the townhouse.

"We are home!" He announced.

Sandrene looked around. It was beautiful and airy in shades of grey and white. Splashes of color came from the curtains and cushions and paintings. It was perfect.

She must have said it out loud.

Saint nodded. "It's all your doing. You decorated it yourself. You went furniture shopping with Shawn. You dictated where you wanted everything."

"Shawn?" Sandrene furrowed your brow. "One of your brothers?"

"No," Saint sighed, "my sister-in-law. She is married to Jordan, my brother."

"Sorry," Sandrene said sheepishly, "I don't remember any of this."

"I understand," Saint said, "don't push yourself. I should tell them not to come over."

"No, don't." Sandrene sat in one of the plush sofas. "I can handle this."

Preston was the first to come over followed closely by his family.

Preston's wife, Sheryl, introduced her and then hugged her

with friendly familiarity.

"Poor baby, I can't remember parts of my past, and they are never going to come back but you, you will remember, don't give up hope."

"You couldn't remember?" Sandrene frowned. "Why?"

"I was in an accident." Sheryl shrugged. "You know the story already. When you remember we'll compare notes."

"Aunty Sands, it's me, Pete." A young man who looked just like Preston came over to her. "I am happy you were found. I mean this. Every night since we heard that you and Uncle Saint were not doing well, Daddy has us praying that you two will find your way back together. It's amazing how God answered the prayer, isn't it?"

"Don't inundate her with too much info, Pete," Preston said. He shook her hand politely.

"Sandrene, we are happy that you are back."

Pretty soon the living room was filled with the Wiley brothers and their wives. It was a little overwhelming.

Sandrene had to be reintroduced to each of them and endure their sympathies.

They asked her about her time in Limestone Hill, and they listened with different levels of horror as she told them her daily routine.

"That place sounds worse than the Rio Grande Valleys," Lucia, Guy's wife said. "At least we had electricity in our section of the valleys."

"Not where Micky lives," Guy murmured. "It sounds like my summers with Micky."

"Who is Micky?" Sandrene asked puzzled.

And then they remembered that she had no memory and apologized profusely. It seemed as if they were always apologizing. She was not the Sandrene that they knew, without her memories. She just listened to them. As far as she was concerned, they were a bunch of strangers discussing other strangers.

She wanted to escape them.

Saint seemed to sense her disquiet because he was looking at her wilting. He stood up to tell them goodbye when somebody opened the door.

There was the click-click of heels on the marble tiles, and a voice that sounded exactly like hers said, "Oh, you are all here!"

****

The room stilled. Even Saint looked as if he was unsure what to do.

"So, let me get this straight." The woman who looked just like her came into the family circle and looked around. "You are having a family party without me. Go figure, the last four months you have all been acting as if I am no longer a part of your little clan."

"Gracie," Saint gritted his teeth, "what are you doing here?"

"Nuh uh," she wagged her finger at Saint. "I am Sandrene, your wife. I lived here until a few weeks ago when you kicked me out. I see you are all fawning over Gracie, sucking up her little sympathy play while she acts like me."

"Wait a minute," Saint shook his head. "Gracie, you have a lot to answer for. I can't believe you think that you are going to get away with this."

"That's right, Gracie has a lot to answer for. I was talking to her lawyer friend today and yesterday. He said that Gracie wanted to escape her life and she plotted to get away from it all by shacking up with Benjamin up in the hills.

"By the way, I called Benjamin's mother, so sorry to hear of her loss."

Saint was speechless. "Gracie come on. This is not going to hold up to scrutiny."

"Stop calling me Gracie. My name is Sandrene Hope Russell Wiley. I am the sister that you married. These last couple of months have been hell. I had a miscarriage. I had a business to run. I had a marriage that had taken a turn for the worst because my husband didn't want me anymore and now he is messing with my sister.

"And you are all in on it." She pointed at the family members.

"When Gracie is over her innocent amnesia act, and you rediscover what sympathy is, I will be at Gracie's apartment. It's only fitting since she is taking up my space here. She turned to Sandrene. "You are welcome to come. It is your place. I am your sister, and I love you, even after all you've done."

"I... I..." Sandrene was at a loss for words. "I am Gracie? Not Sandrene?"

"That's right." Gracie sneered. "Don't let them poison your mind. I have the truth."

"Sandrene don't listen to her. She is a liar." Saint was exasperated with Gracie's latest stunt.

"Stop calling her, Sandrene," Gracie hissed. "I am your wife and if you are so gung-ho about her being me, test our DNA."

"I already did," Saint growled. "You have identical DNA. Regular DNA testing cannot distinguish you two apart. You know that, did your lawyer friend put you up to this one man show?"

"Lawyer friend? You mean Gracie's off and on lover, Jason? I met with him to discuss the divorce. He convinced me to give us another try."

"I think you should know that a buddy of mine in Germany

will be running further tests on your genome. It should be conclusive."

"Good." Gracie snorted. "Until then, I want her out of my house. She has a perfectly good apartment to live in. I don't want her here with you. You are already lusting after my sister. If you ask me, this is low, Saint."

Saint groaned. "Stop this, Gracie."

"You always desired Gracie and tried to hide it." Gracie grinned. "You want her because she is the adventurous twin."

"Get out." Saint hissed.

"Not until I am good and ready. This is my matrimonial home. Gracie is back, and her apartment is waiting."

"So help me, Gracie," Saint murmured. "What's wrong with you. After all, you have done, you don't have a hint of remorse? Instead, you are still acting like your sister. I can't fathom what kind of diabolical mind could do this."

"I decided that I want to fight for our marriage even if you do not, and if calling me Gracie makes you feel better, I am sorry for you, Saint. Let me go get my things."

Gracie looked back at Sandrene. "Maybe I should take you home. I don't want you here."

"She is not going anywhere," Saint hissed. "Why do you desperately want her to leave with you so that you can hurt her again? Haven't you done enough?

"Well, I am not going anywhere either, at least not for tonight." Gracie headed up the stairs.

"Wait!" Saint called before she left.

"When is our wedding date?"

"The first one or the second one? Dec 12 and May 3. You still haven't told your brothers yet that we eloped at the beach house in Portland because we couldn't wait.

"And while we are playing twenty questions, you have a heart-shaped birthmark on your lower right shoulder. I call you Green Eyes for a pet name. I love to bake pastries but not a fan of sugary treats. There are a million and one things only you and I know because we have been together for so long. You love me not her.

"We'll find it again, Saint. Please don't project your feelings for me on my sister she wanted to escape, and she did. Now she can't remember a thing and you are making her out to be me. That's not right."

Chapter Twenty

"What are you going to do?" Preston was the first to ask after Gracie left the stunned audience behind.

"Sandrene had a miscarriage?" Sheryl asked almost at the same time. "Why didn't she tell me, we were pretty close."

"No, she didn't." Saint sighed. "That piece of information is just to add intrigue to Gracie's lies.

"Which one is Gracie, and which is Sandrene?" Shawn demanded. "How can you even tell now?"

"You got married twice, dude." Case interjected, "and never told any of us? I told you about mine."

"Hold on," Jordan glared at Case, "you are married?"

"And you didn't say anything?" Preston glowered at Case. "When did this happen?"

"It was six years ago in Cuba," Case looked cornered. "It was supposed to be a rescue."

Everybody wanted to hear more, and they turned to Case to spill his story.

After they got all the details they could from Case, Aisha was the one who turned back to Saint.

"How would Fake Sandrene know these things about you? Unless she is the real Sandrene?"

"Because Real Sandrene has diaries," Sheryl chipped in. "She had stacks of diaries that she has kept from childhood. She wrote everything down. I always envied her dedication to that."

"It's not something to envy if you have an evil twin," Shawn murmured. "It's like giving her the blueprint for your life. She would just slip effortlessly into your shoes, knowing all your secrets."

" And now we can't tell them apart because this Sandrene has no memory and the other Sandrene probably knows every single intimate detail about her."

They all turned to look at Sandrene who was listening to them with a bemused expression on her face.

"Sorry, I can't help with this mystery."

"I think we should all leave," Jordan said, "and give Saint space to work this out without an audience."

"But how is he going to tell who is the right one?" Shawn asked.

"Anyone who he is sexually attracted to is Sandrene for him." Walter chipped in. "But I don't think you should sleep with any of them at this point. Your wires could be crossed and if you end up with Gracie. It would be..."

"Adultery?" Aisha piped in.

"Yes, but I was thinking disaster," Walter said.

Saint looked at Sandrene after Aisha said that. She immediately froze. That was her concern too.

She looked like a cornered animal as if the wolves were out to get her.

"You are just going to have to wait this out until Sandrene

or er Gracie gets her memory back."

"She is Sandrene, not Gracie," Saint said exasperatedly.

"He has two wives," Shawn murmured. "Two Sandrenes."

"No, I don't." Saint hissed. "I have one Sandrene."

"We'll pray for you." Preston squeezed his hand when leaving.

"Likewise," Jordan looked at him solemnly. "You sure you can manage okay. We are here for you, you know that."

Saint nodded. "I know."

When he was finally alone with Sandrene. He found her in the corner of the settee her eyes awash with tears.

"Hey," he walked over to her. "Don't cry. We'll get to the bottom of this, I promise."

"But what if I am not your wife? She husked. "What if what she said was true? Maybe I took those memory inhibitors to escape my life."

Saint pulled her to him and hugged her tight. "No, I know you. I would know you in the dark with a thousand other women around. Trust me, on this."

****

"She is the imposter. I am Sandrene." Gracie paced from one end of the living room to another. Mom, Dad, help me out here."

Sanya and Lamar blinked rapidly confusion stamped on their faces.

Saint heaved a sigh. The parents were not sure who was who and Sandrene was no help. She couldn't remember a thing. She had not recognized her parents when they walked through the front door moments earlier, frantic with worry.

She had made an effort with her parents, but they were strangers to her. She was looking at them now in fascination.

She was sitting in the corner of the settee like a shadow, unsure about where she fit in and who she was.

Saint's heart reached out to her. He was the only one out of everybody in the world who knew that she was his Sandrene. It was a sobering thought.

Gracie was in fine form. She was playing the role for all she was worth, spreading doubt everywhere even with her own parents.

Saint could see it on their faces. As they looked between Gracie and Sandrene and then back again.

Sanya started firing off questions, the answers would be things that only she and Sandrene would know, and Gracie answered easily. Even affecting a wounded look in her eyes.

"I can't believe this, mom. Gracie is taking everything from me. She has Saint protecting her. My husband is on my sister's side. They even slept together last night in our matrimonial bed."

"No, we did not." Saint was forced to defend himself. "I slept in the guest room. Sandrene requested that. She doesn't want to sleep with a married man. That alone, without her memory, tells me that she is not you, Gracie. You would not mind that at all. Would you?"

"Stop calling me, Gracie. It hurts, Saint. How can you be so brainwashed?"

He saw the doubt gathering in Sanya's eyes. "When will this thing wear off?"

"The doctor's estimate within three months to a year. They have never administered the doses so close together. They have no reference for this kind of case."

"And her brain, when it's done?" Sanya asked fearfully.

"Apparently it will be as normal." Saint grimaced. "This is not permanent. They are working on a version of the medication that will have a longer effect, but thankfully this batch was not it."

"Thank you, Jesus," Sanya said. She went over to her daughter.

"Honey, I love you. It pains me that you don't know who I am."

But you don't know who she is either. Saint wanted to point out. He held his peace.

"She loves the attention so much when it wears off, she won't admit it," Gracie growled. "She will pretend as if she is innocent to all of this and she will act as if she is me. This is awful, Mom. I mean, I thought that Saint and I had some hiccups these last couple of months, but to see him transferring his affections to Gracie, and calling her his wife, and treating her like he used to treat me... I can't deal with this."

"You are very good. Excellent," Saint looked at Gracie scornfully. "Unbelievable!"

"Saint, is this true?" Sanya queried desperately. "I am confused."

"I am not." Saint looked at Gracie dispassionately. "This is a good act, but it is still an act. She had me fooled for four months. I thought Sandrene had changed. I thought she was overworked. I thought so many things, and then I found my real wife and then I knew."

"I had a miscarriage. I didn't tell anybody about it." Gracie hissed. "Forgive me if I was not acting all lovey-dovey and sweet. I was crushed. I was dealing with something bad alone, and I was angry and bitter."

"You blanked Matthew's wife, Abby." Saint pointed out.

"Because I no longer had any free time to be having lunch and talking nonsense about harvest programs and church potlucks. I didn't blank her. Told her I was busy."

"Your employees are calling you Gangrene Sandrene!"

Saint hissed.

"Because they are a bunch of children who think that because I am easy going and cool that they can give me mediocre work because I am the only one in charge. By the way, Chef Brown was the one who started that name because I told him what to do. I didn't allow him to bully me like he does my parents. When I am in charge, I am in charge. I know a little bit more about food and what works with the customers than he does, and it is paying off. The change in menu is drawing in an even larger crowd."

What about our sex life? Explain that away. Saint wanted to shout. Explain why I am no longer attracted to you.

He didn't bother.

Gracie looked at them mournfully and then grabbed her handbag. "I don't want to seem heartless, but I don't want this fake Sandrene here in my house. She stayed with us before, and it put a wedge between us."

Gracie's eyes teared up, and she wiped away the tears impatiently. "I have to get to work. I hired a new manager yesterday."

"We are here now," Lamar said heavily. "The load will be significantly reduced for you at work. Just give us a couple of hours. We'll be there to help out."

"Thank you, Dad. I will be back here later." Gracie looked at Saint mournfully.

"You moved out." Saint pointed out. "You said you hated it here. You wanted to see other people, and you wanted a divorce."

Sandrene gasped.

"Yes, that's right," Saint looked over at her, "while Gracie was pretending to be you and living here she wanted to break up our marriage, and I almost fell for it."

"Rubbish," Gracie scorned. "I still want a divorce especially now when you have switched your affections to my sister."

Saint shook his head. "You can't do this, Gracie. I didn't marry you. I can't divorce you."

"I am Sandrene, and I will do it Jason said I can apply now."

"The law requires a year of separation," Saint said.

"But there are special considerations, and it can be arranged. Jason is in my corner." Gracie hissed. "I am applying for the divorce today."

When she left Sanya got up and hugged Saint.

"I am so sorry about this. I used to put nail polish on the bottom of their feet to tell them apart, red for Sandrene, blue for Gracie."

"When they were growing up, it was easy to tell them apart by their temperament. Gracie was the fussy one, Sandrene the calm one. And then Gracie had her spectacular rebellious years and we kind of accepted that volatility was going to be part and parcel of who she was.

"Seeing that one daughter can't remember anything and can't refute what is happening, I do not know what to tell you, Saint. I simply cannot tell them apart. If Gracie is parading around as Sandrene, she is doing it really well and really convincingly."

Lamar sighed. "We can't claim parental discernment, but maybe Sandrene is right."

"Gracie," Saint said through gritted teeth, "or Fake Sandrene."

Lamar sighed heavily. "Maybe Fake Sandrene is right, and Real Sandrene should come and live with us for the time being. Just until she gets her memory back. Things will be much easier on the home front."

"I am not letting my wife go and then let Gracie win," Saint said stubbornly. "She is a deceiver. She wants our marriage to fail. It's her revenge. She wants to keep me and Sandrene apart, and you guys are buying it, lapping up her acting and her lies. I can tell them apart. I may not have known what Gracie was up to a couple of months ago, but the moment Sandrene left this house, I knew that she was replaced. "

"I couldn't pinpoint how but I knew that the woman here wasn't my wife. I didn't understand my reaction then, but I understand now, and I am fighting every attempt to keep us apart.

"I lost her four months ago, and I am not letting another day go by with us apart. I love her with everything I have."

Lamar nodded. "Okay, Sir. Your call. "

"Now I understand why I never even felt a pang when Gracie was going on and on about a divorce. It didn't move me because I didn't love her. If Sandrene said something like that it would have torn me apart."

Chapter Twenty-One

By the end of the week and several sleepless nights, Saint was ready for answers on how to deal with Gracie. He was finding it impossible to sleep now that Sandrene was waking up at four o'clock and pacing the house.

She had gotten accustomed to getting up early and going to the farm, she told him apologetically. She couldn't stay in bed too late. She didn't have to say it, but she felt like a caged creature. She couldn't go to the restaurant, Gracie was there. She had nothing to do, and she felt overwhelmed when she met people who were supposed to be her friends, but she had no clue who they were. And she didn't want to go on holiday with Saint. Basically, she was a shadow of the wife he knew, a stranger who he had to woo all over again.

After a few days, he called Guy. He had planned to take some time away anyway and have Sandrene get to know him all over again.

Since Sandrene was used to the farming lifestyle, and

Guy's place was perfect for that, he would take her there.

She squealed with joy when he told her and started packing quickly. "Can we leave now?"

Saint was conflicted when he said yes. He wanted to stay and fight Gracie. He couldn't let her continue with her manipulations, but he saw how unhappy Sandrene looked cooped up in the townhouse like a caged animal.

The drive up to Guy's was mostly silent. She fell asleep as soon as they were on their way. It was such a deep sleep that the various bumps and rolls from the road did not have an impact on her.

She woke up and looked around when they were near Guy's place and sighed. "I love the country air. It's calming."

Saint nodded. "It is."

"Guy said to remind you that September and October is planting season and you will be worked if you really want to be."

"I want to be." Sandrene looked out the window. Guy's place was huge. She knew the exact moment they started on his property, the road got smoother, and there was a sign that said: To the Strawberry Farm.

They were greeted at the main farmhouse by Guy's wife, Lucia. Guy was on the east side attending to business.

They were shown to a two-bedroom guest suite. Lucia looked at him with sympathy in her eyes as she pointed out the adjoining bedroom doors.

"I will survive," Saint said under his breath.

Lucia gave him a glimmer of a smile. "Would you like a light lunch? Dinner is at five."

"No thanks," Sandrene said wandering onto the patio in the room she chose. "I love it here!"

"Me too." Lucia nodded, "when I first came here I was in amazement. I have so many pictures of everything. Every day there is something new."

They chatted with Lucia for a while. When she left Saint joined Sandrene on the patio.

Sandrene studied him closely, her eyes running over every feature as if committing them to memory. He endured the scrutiny. He turned and studied her right back.

"Saint Wiley," she finally said in the silence.

"Sandrene Wiley." He responded just as somberly.

"You are the only one who believes that I am Sandrene."

"I do. I have no doubt that you are."

"No doubt at all?" Sandrene raised an eyebrow. "Not even a teensy bit?"

"None," Saint watched her, "not even fifty look-alikes can fool me. What I am wondering now is, how am I going to get you to fall in love with me again?"

Sandrene stared at him in awe. "I don't think you will have to try at all. I can't believe that you love me. I look in the mirror, I am nothing special, and you are...you."

Saint frowned at her, "You are more special to me than anything, even my life. I would do anything for you. Until you, I never knew what true love was."

Sandrene gasped. "Well, I don't know what to say."

Saint smiled. "If you had your memories you would say you love me just as much. If the shoe were on the other foot, you would fight as hard to be with me. We have something special, and I want it back with or without your memories. I know it won't be easy adjusting, but I am a patient man."

"Tell me about our marriage." Sandrene looked away from him and into the view below. "How were we together? What was our routine like?"

"Great." Saint sighed, "I miss that. Some days we went to badminton or tennis together in the mornings. Then we'd go to work; sometimes we'd meet for lunch. In the evenings we usually hang out at home, though you oversee a lot of functions. You said if you never attended another party you would be fine. The weekends were ours though. We have lots and lots of sex."

Sandrene giggled. "Really now?"

"You are insatiable." Saint shook his head. "I can barely keep up."

"Stop it." Sandrene laughed.

"Seriously." Saint took her hands in his and dropped a kiss on her upturned palm. "For some reason, that gesture turns you on. It's the strangest thing."

Sandrene tightened her hands around his and then moved into his arms. "I feel a strange tingle everywhere."

"Told you." Saint kissed her all the way up her arm.

"I am going to trust you, Saint." Sandrene closed her eyes. "I don't think you'll have to try too hard for me to love you again. I am already halfway there."

Saint cupped her face; his hands gently caressed her cheeks.

Tears welled. She was so very lucky. Who would have thought that her life would end up like this, a beautiful man, declaring his undying love and swearing that she felt the same.

"Hey," Saint whispered, "no crying. Just loving."

She pressed her mouth to his. The kiss was electrifying. She clung to Saint as if he were her lifeline, the only one who knew her, and he clung to her as if he never wanted to let her go. She was the one who led him to the bed.

****

"You two are acting like newlyweds," Guy mocked Saint. "You are worse than Lucia and me and we are the newlyweds."

Saint chuckled. The four of them were in the kitchen having dinner together. Catherine, Guy's helper had the day off.

Sandrene had volunteered to cook. They sat at the farmer's table and chatted. Lucia had enlarged some of her photos to be framed and was asking their opinion.

"Hey, I like that one." Sandrene pointed to a bowl of strawberries with the water still evident on their skin. "Look at the detail on them. It's amazing."

"And though they closely look alike," Guy said proudly, "not one of them is the same, different taste even though they may taste the same, no two strawberries are exactly alike. They have different number of seeds on the skin too. You see, unlike berries, they wear their seed on the outside. Each strawberry seed is considered to be its own separate fruit. I would challenge anyone to find the same number of seeds on two strawberries. It's amazing how everything that God makes, no matter how insignificant you may think it is, has its own uniqueness. Every strawberry in that bowl is unique."

"Goodness don't let him get started," Saint muttered. "He has strawberry fever."

Lucia grinned. "Leave my hubby alone. I love his farm lessons."

"So, what's the lesson here?" Saint started grinning and then stopped. "Oh my God, you are right!"

"I am?" Guy frowned, "about what?"

"Every creature is unique!"

"That's right, you know that." Guy raised an eyebrow, "but carry on."

"How are identical twins unique? Not DNA, not unless you can afford a thorough expensive test that will thoroughly search for differences in the genome, but fingerprints!"

Saint grinned. "Every single created thing on this planet is unique."

Sandrene gave him a thumbs up. "That's right."

"I am going to need more than your thumbs honey. I am going to need all of your fingers too. And Gracie's. Then we'll compare them to the ones we have on file in our fingerprint ID system."

"I am happy a humble farmer such as myself could have inspired this moment," Guy said grinning.

"You are a genius, and I could kiss you," Saint said heading for his brother.

"Please don't," Guy said getting up.

"Why not?" Saint laughed wickedly.

He got up and ran, and Saint went after him. Lucia and Sandrene doubled over in laughter.

Chapter Twenty-Two

Two weeks later, his first day back at the office, nothing much had changed. Gracie was still doing her Sandrene act.

Sandrene was still without her memory. Saint was sitting at his desk half listening as his secretary, Julian ran through his high pile of correspondence.

And then she handed him a pink perfumed envelop with his name on it.

"The bearer from the Waterfalls dropped that off."

Saint grunted and pushed it away to almost the edge of his desk.

Julian chuckled. "Your sister-in-law still running amok?"

"I haven't heard that term in a while." Saint smiled. "But amok it is. She is having a field day being Fake Sandrene."

"Maybe you should check what the card says," Julian suggested curiously. "I saw the bearer with others for your brothers."

"Really?" Saint picked up the pink envelop and read with

disbelieving eyes.

Divorce Party. I Do. I Did. I am Done. Please join Sandrene Hope Russell as she closes one chapter of her life and begin another. Drinks, food, karaoke, galore at the Waterfalls this Saturday night at eight in the courtyard.

He read it out loud and slowly.

Julian nodded. "So, are you going?"

"Oh yes." Saint nodded. "I am going, and I am taking my wife with me. Why not? It's our divorce party."

"This is the strangest thing..." Julian shook her head. "If someone had told me about it I would say this is make believe."

Saint looked over the invitation again and then started laughing. "Now why would you invite your supposed husband to your divorce party? I don't know what Gracie is up to, but I am here for it."

"Boss," Garland barged into the office. "I got it! Got Gracie's prints, and matched the results. We had to retake this a few times because she was not cooperating with our methods. I had to enlist Chef Brown to help me, and he got perfect prints. He had her put her hand in a mold."

"Excuse me," Julian said and left while Garland came into the office with a huge smile on his bearded face.

"I don't know why I never enlisted Chef Brown's help before. He said he figured out that Gracie was an imposter a long time ago and he was concerned about Sandrene. He said he didn't know who to tell about his suspicions."

"I set him straight. He was happy to help and guess what?"

"The fingerprints matched the ones we have of Gracie on the database." Saint smiled.

"Oh yes." Garland nodded.

"Thank you, God, and thank you, Matthew," Saint said fervently. "He was the one who came up with the idea to implement a fingerprinting ID system at the Waterfalls as an extra security measure."

Garland grinned. "I am happy that this is sorted. When are you going to set the police on Gracie?"

"A part of me wanted to know how far she would go with this." Saint mused. "I wanted to see when her conscience or human decency would chip in, but I am cordially invited to her divorce party, so I was thinking since she is making a public spectacle of my marriage, I am going to respond in kind."

****

The Waterfalls was decorated in white, gray and silver, their wedding colors. The irony was not lost on Saint.

Gracie was dressed in a clingy silver dress with a plunging neckline. It was a packed house.

She had invited quite a few of Sandrene's friends and associates, even his brothers. She wanted this to be public; she wanted it to be known that she was finished with the marriage. She wanted to destroy her sister's happiness so bad it was actually sad.

Saint had fielded the concern from several friends, but he encouraged them to come along. All his brothers were there. Even Case had flown in from Cayman to see the showdown.

There were many bewildered expressions on the people's faces when they saw the Wiley brothers and their wives arriving.

Saint was dressed in black from head to toe, Sandrene was in white, and they entered the venue a little before eight.

Lamar greeted them at the door. "Saint, we tried to convince her not to do this. I wanted to avoid all of this and do it quietly. We have our lawyer on standby nevertheless.

She is still our child."

"I know." Saint nodded.

Lamar hugged Sandrene. "No progress on the memories yet Sandy? Your mother and I miss you."

Sandrene hugged him back. "No progress, but at least I know for sure who I am and that gives me great joy."

They had intended to make a grand entrance, but Gracie was in her element and was singing karaoke at the front of the room.

She stopped mid-song and chuckled ladies and gentlemen. "My cheating husband and my sister, Gracie."

Everybody turned to look at him and Sandrene.

"Now you all know why I am having this divorce party." Gracie announced at the front of the room.

"I am going to wring her neck," Preston whispered under his breath.

"No need for violence." Saint chuckled. "She is going to get what is coming to her."

He walked up to the microphone with Sandrene beside him, taking it from Gracie's hand. "Friends, colleagues and family, I permitted this party and even invited some of you that were not on the guest list to come to Gracie's Divorce Party because I needed you all here together to explain."

Gracie tried to take the microphone back from him, but two police officers who were standing by held her back.

"You will listen, madam," One of them said forcefully.

"Nearly seven months ago, Gracie decided to switch places with her sister..."

You could hear a pin drop. Somebody had turned off the karaoke machine.

"She paid a worker here to kidnap my wife and drug her with an experimental drug that can wipe memories. Now if you think that this sounds like a movie plot, you are right..."

Chuckles from the audience broke up the solemnity of his statement.

"I am Sandrene," Gracie hissed.

"These fingerprints say you are not," Saint smirked holding up the fingerprint results.

Gracie widened her eyes in horror. "How did you get my fingerprints?"

"I helped with that, Two Faced Sandrea Grace." Chef Brown snickered. "I knew you weren't Sandrene from the very first day you waltzed in here giving orders. Sandrene always uses polite words, like please and thank you. Keep that in mind if you want to impersonate her next time."

"I hate you." Gracie started struggling with the police. "And you too Sandrene and mom and dad and especially you, Saint. I hate all of you! I never got a fair chance. You couldn't have given me a fair chance to be her! You are all pigs!"

The police carted her off after reading her rights. Saint and Sandrene stayed behind for the party.

Epilogue

Sandrene didn't get her memory back fully until February the next year. By then she was six months pregnant.

"My divorce party baby." She grinned and rubbed her belly.

It was a relief to remember everyone and to feel normal again. Well, as normal as one could feel when she was carrying identical twin girls.

She was back at work. Chef Brown had redubbed her Serene Sandrene. Saint found the nickname laughable because she was not a serene pregnant lady. She had moments of panic when she thought about her identical twin girls.

"Suppose they are not close?" She fretted after they had gotten back the 3D pictures of the babies. She looked at them while they lounged in the living room.

"Suppose we stop worrying, Serene Sandrene?" Saint got up and kissed her on the forehead. "They'll be fine. Just keep them away from their aunt, Gracie. Let her be a distant aunt who only sends cards every Christmas."

Gracie had gotten two years suspended sentence for a host of charges, kidnapping, identity theft, paying for stolen goods. The judge had been lenient, and her lawyer, Jason Lynch had fought quite hard on her behalf.

She had moved to Montego Bay to start afresh shortly after her case was heard. She left Sandrene's diaries with her parents and a note attached to the bundle of books which said: I am sorry, Sandrene. I hope you will find it in your heart to forgive. I am working on being a better person.

Sandrene had a feeling that she would do it too. She surprisingly had no ill will toward Gracie. She just thought that they needed the distance between them. Time would tell how they'd end up.

She glanced at Saint and grinned. "Hey, Green Eyes. Your children are kicking."

Saint came over to her and put his hand on her riotous belly and grinned at her too.

The knock on the door broke up the moment.

"I'll get that," Saint said kissing her wiggling belly.

"I am on my way out. I could have called, but I saw your car in the driveway. " Preston removed his shades. "I want you to do a thorough background check for me."

"On who?" Saint raised an eyebrow.

"A young lady who is applying to work in my office for the summer."

"I had no idea you did thorough background checks on summer workers?" Saint frowned.

"Oh yes I do, when the summer worker's name is Lyla Wiley."

"Lyla Wiley as in Case's er...wife."

"That's right." Preston put his shades back on. "I know you'll do a thorough job."

Saint nodded. "You bet on it."

He headed back into the house. Sandrene smiled at him. "Come here Green Eyes, let's snuggle together."

"What a great offer." Saint grinned. "The best I have heard all day."

Continure reading for an excerpt from
A Case of Love (Wiley Brothers Book 6)

"Lyla Wiley! I have been calling your name for the past fifteen minutes."

Lyla jumped. Brandi had unceremoniously pulled out her headphones and was talking loudly in her ear.

"But I should have known that you would be over here drooling over C. Wiley. You are so predictable. Girl, you have it bad."

Lyla dragged her eyes from her computer screen and focused on her roommate.

"What is it?"

Brandi grinned and waved two envelops in the air. "Nothing! Just the fact that we got in! We got in! We both got in!"

Lyla got up and squealed. "Yes!"

Brandi grabbed her, and they danced around the living room and then collapsed in hysterics in the overstuffed sofas.

"You are really related to the Wileys?" Brandi looked at her, a dazed expression in her eyes. "I never believed you did until now. I always thought you were just pulling my leg."

"I am a relative in a way, a distant way," Lyla said, pushing her hair from her eyes. "I was just as anxious as you to see if I would get in."

"Who would have thunk it?" Brandi got up, her energy restored, and headed for her phone, "Brandi Phillips, management trainee. I have got to tell my mom. I can't believe that I am going to be working in the offices of Preston Wiley. I'll be there the entire summer as a management trainee. Five months of training, whoop! Whoop!

"My mother is not going to believe this." Brandi slapped her forehead and then handed her an envelope. "Sorry, here is your acceptance letter. Look at the pay. Look at it!"

Lyla took the letter from Brandi and swallowed the lecture that was on the tip of her tongue about privacy.

It would not make a difference. It would sail straight over Brandi's head. It was a good thing that she rarely received regular mail.

She grabbed her computer and found that Wiley Supermarket had written her via email too. She read the mail while Brandi gushed to her mother over the phone.

She tried to ignore Brandi, only tuning in when she heard her name.

"It has to be Lyla pulling strings on the quiet, Mom. You know Wiley Supermarkets was a long shot. They do not usually take third-year students in their management trainee batch. I put Lyla as one of my references, and I got in."

Lyla watched Brandi enviously. She had a close relationship with her mother and a close-knit family.

Lyla had no one to call. She didn't have a family. Contrary to Brandi's assumptions that she had some sort of influence on the Wiley's she had none. She stalked them on the internet, she pored over articles in which they were mentioned, and she watched any and every music video that was released by C. Wiley.

She had no more influence than a regular fangirl.

She knew nothing more about the Wiley's than what they wanted the world to know. In the past she had badgered Sienna, her former guardian about Case, but Sienna only knew what her son Jules told her and that was not much.

Lyla suddenly missed Sienna. She had been the only mother figure in her whole life. She was nurturing, caring, and a true mother earth type who embraced everyone and loved all people and then cancer took her.

She hadn't been diagnosed long before and then three months later she was gone.

Lyla sighed. She was alone. If she didn't get the deposits in her account every month and her school fees paid, no questions asked, she would even believe that Case had forgotten about her too.

But as it was, she was well provided for. If she wanted anything extra she called Rita Bloom, the lawyer in charge of Case Wiley's affairs, that is what Sienna had done when she was alive.

Lyla had to reluctantly make a call in her second year of university when Sienna had died, and she had nowhere to live.

Rita was efficient and brisk. She had been the one to help her set up her personal accounts. She had been the one who had found the two-bedroom furnished apartment that was a ten-minute drive from school and had supplied her with Brandi as a roommate.

Lyla had no idea how the apartment was paid for. She didn't pay rent or utilities. Case was her silent benefactor.

No expense was to be speared where she was concerned. She switched screens from her email account to look at his music video again.

She knew each of his features well. She was obsessed with him. She had been since she was fourteen years old and saw him first in Havana.

He had been on stage, singing, My God is Awesome in Spanish, and she had felt every word.

She had fantasies of them meeting again now when she was an adult, of him falling in love with her and the two of them living as man and wife in the true sense.

Impossible dreams.

Case had saved her from a fate worse than death. Her mother would have sold her to Casa de Prostituta and Havana's most notorious pimp if Case had not been moved to help her out.

She again hit play on My God Is Awesome video and

listened to Case's smooth rendition of the song.

"Can't you give the guy a rest for three minutes." Brandi chuckled. She had finished with her phone call.

"I know he looks good, but he is unattainable. Focus on the men in your real life. Do you know how many guys on the university campus would give their left arm to go out with you? But you ignore them all."

Lyla grimaced. "I am not interested in the social scene until I graduate."

"You are exasperating." Brandi sat beside her and glanced at the screen. "Take out the headphones. I want to hear him sing."

Lyla grinned. "You like him too."

"His voice is like honey, and his face." Brandi fanned herself. "Ooh, child. When I see him in videos, I think, glory. No man looks this good in real life. He is probably short and has a bad temper."

"He is not short," Lyla said contemplatively. "He is tall, with skin like dark honey, the warmest kindest eyes, covered with eyelashes like fans and the gentlest smile. He is gorgeous and humble at the same time."

"I want to see if this is true." Brandi grinned, "We should go to his concert in Negril tomorrow."

"Negril?" Lyla raised an eyebrow.

"Yes, why not?" Brandi put on her determined face. "Adam has tickets. We can stay at his friend, Jerry's house, and then come back on Sunday, have a road trip weekend."

"I hate going out with you and Adam. I hate being the third wheel."

"But you will do it because you want to see Mr. Handsome live." Brandi grinned cheekily. "Maybe we can even act as total groupies and go and see him backstage. Who knows? Maybe you can pretend that you two are related, you have that Wiley name, it seems to open doors."

OTHER BOOKS BY BRENDA BARRETT

Pryce Sisters Series

Baby For A Pryce (Book 1)- Giselle Pryce had a bright future, two scholarships from Ivy League schools and a track career that was going somewhere, when she discovered she was pregnant. She had several decisions to make.

Right Pryce Wrong Time (Book 2)- Tiana got her high school teacher James fired for inappropriate conduct because of her jealousy. When she meets him again as an adult in a different situation, she has no idea how to act.

Yours, For A Pryce (Book 3)- Toddy Pryce offers his favorite sister Elsa to his young political rival Mason Magnus in exchange to not run against him in the next elections.

Wiley Brothers Series

Between Brothers (Book 0)- The beginning of the Wiley brothers saga, Joseph Wiley's unconventional family life may prove to be fatal to some members of the family.

For Pete's Sake (Book 1)- Preston has a run in with a child named Pete who claims that he is the grandson of their former housekeeper Pamela Stone.

Crossing Jordan (Book 2)- Jordan is miffed when Shawn takes her new fiancé to Jamaica and insists that he be man of honor at their wedding.

Fire and Walter (Book 3)- Walter's past came rushing to greet him shortly after his appointment as church elder. The new pastor was his childhood molestor, his wife was his ex from college and her cousin was the girl who got away. Walter had a lot of decisions to make.

The Perfect Guy (Book 4) - After a patient five years waiting for Lucia, Guy had his work cut out for him to prove himself worthy of her affections. He had played the part of poor farmer for too long and now he had competition in the form of the handsome doctor Ace Jackson.

The Patience of A Saint (Book 5)- Something was wrong with Saint's wife Sandrene. It didn't take a genius to see that she was changed beyond all recognition. Saint had to get to the bottom of it, before it was too late for them to salvage anything from the relationship.

A Case of Love (Book 6)- After a concert, Case is offered a girl to buy. Her fate was in his hands. He could keep her or leave her to the mercy of her evil family.

Resetter Series

Never Too Late (Book 1)- Addi finds out she is a resetter and goes back to the summer of 92 to change her family's lives.

Never Say Never (Book 2)- Skyler's handsome college lecturer, who happens to be her neighbor, has a 't' in his palms. Should she tell him the significance of it. If she does, would he believe her?

Now or Never (Book 3)- Ten years later Addi and Randy meet again at Randy's engagement party. Why is it that the chemistry between them was still so potent? Can they ever have a future together? Would Randy choose her this time around?

Almost Never (Book 4)- Tech genius Joshua Porter had all but given up on love. He then meets Portia, an inmate at the female penitentiary and his life takes a turn for the adventurous.

The Scarlett Family Series

Scarlett Baby (Book 1)- When the head of the Scarlett family died, Yuri had to return home to Treasure Beach for the funeral. What he didn't count on was seeing Marla, his childhood sweetheart and his best friend's wife. And when emotions overwhelm them and a few months later Marla is pregnant, Yuri wants the impossible: his best friend's wife and the baby they made together...

Scarlett Sinner (Book 2)- Pastor Troy Scarlett realizes the hard way that some sins are bound to be revealed, like the child that he had out of wedlock with his wife's mortal enemy from college. His wife Chelsea was not happy with the status quo. She was not taking care of the son of the woman she had so despised from college. And she could not get over the deep betrayal that she felt from her husband's indiscretion.

Scarlett Secret (Book 3)- Terri Scarlett had a soft spot for her friend, Lola. She was funny and sweet and they looked remarkably alike. But when Lola's Arab prince demands his bride, Terri foolishly exchange places with her friend and they meet up on a world of trouble.

Scarlett Love (Book 4)- Slater always looked forward to delivering packages to the law firm where he could get a glimpse of the stunning female lawyer, Amoy Gardener. Unfortunately, for Slater a woman like Amoy would not take him seriously, especially when she found out that he could not read!

Scarlett Promise (Book 5)- Driven by desperation Lisa Barclay decides to make some extra money by prostituting herself after being kicked out in the streets. Her first customer turns out to be a popular government senator and then to her horror he dies...

Scarlett Bride (Book 6)- When Oliver Scarlett's missionary work in the Congo region was coming to an end, he had a decision to make, marry Ashaki Azanga and save her from being the fourth wife to the chief of the village or leave her to her fate and get on with his life...

Scarlett Heart (Book 7)- After receiving a heart transplant shy librarian Noah Scarlett started to take on character traits that were unlike him and he kept dreaming of a girl named Cassandra Green...

Rebound Series

On The Rebound- For Better or Worse, Brandon vowed to stay with Ashley, but when worse got too much he moved out and met Nadine. For the first time in years he felt happy, but then Ashley remembered her wedding vows...

On The Rebound 2- Ashley reinvented herself and was now a first lady in a country church in Primrose Hill, but her obsessed ex friend Regina showed up and started digging into the lives of the saints at church. Somebody didn't like Regina's digging. Someone had secrets that were shocking enough to kill for...

Magnolia Sisters

Dear Mystery Guy (Book 1)- Della Gold details her life in a journal dedicated to a mystery guy. But when fascination turns into obsession she finds herself wanting to learn even more about him but in her pursuit of the mystery guy she begins to learn more about herself...

Bad Girl Blues (Book 2)- Brigid Manderson wanted to go to med school but for the time being she was an escort working for her mother, an ex-prostitute. When her latest customer offers her the opportunity of a lifetime would she take it? Or would she choose the harder path and uncertain love with a Christian guy?

Her Mistaken Dreams (Book 3)- Caitlin Denvers dream guy had serious issues. He has a dead wife in his past and he was the main suspect in her murder. Did he really do it? Or did Caitlin for the first time have a mistaken dream?

Just Like Yesterday (Book 4)- Hazel Brown lost six months of memory including the summer that she conceived her son, and had no idea who his father could be. Now that she had the means to fight to get him back from the Deckers, she finds out that the handsome Curtis Decker is willing to share her son with her after all.

New Song Series

Going Solo (Book 1)- Carson Bell, had a lovely voice, a heart of gold, and was no slouch in the looks department. So why did Alice abandon him and their daughter? What did she want after ten years of silence?

Duet on Fire (Book 2)- Ian and Ruby had problems trying to conceive a child. If that wasn't enough, her ex-lover the current pastor of their church wants her back...

Tangled Chords (Book 3)- Xavier Bell, the poor, ugly duckling has made it rich and his looks have been incredibly improved too. Farrah Knight, hotel heiress had cruelly rejected him in the past but now she needed help. Could Xavier forgive and forget?

Broken Harmony(Book 4)- Aaron Lee, wanted the top job in his family company but he had a moral clause to consider just when Alka, his married ex-girlfriend walks back into his life.

A Past Refrain (Book 5)- Jayce had issues with forgetting Haley Greenwald even though he had a new woman in his life. Will he ever be able to shake his love for Haley?

Perfect Melody (Book 6)- Logan Moore had the perfect wife, Melody but his secretary Sabrina was hell bent on breaking up the family. Sabrina wanted Logan whatever the cost and she had a secret about Melody, that could shatter Melody's image to everyone.

The Bancroft Family Series

Homely Girl (Book 0) - April and Taj were opposites in so many ways. He was the cute, athletic boy that everybody wanted to be friends with. She was the overweight, shy, and withdrawn girl. Do April and Taj have a love that can last a lifetime? Or will time and separate paths rip them apart?

Saving Face (Book 1) - Mount Faith University drama begins with a dead president and several suspects including the president in waiting Ryan Bancroft.

Tattered Tiara (Book 2) - Micah Bancroft is targeted by femme fatale Deidra Durkheim. There are also several rape cases to be solved.

Private Dancer (Book 3) Adrian Bancroft was gutted when he returned to Jamaica and found out that his first and only love Cathy Taylor was a stripper and was literally owned by the menacing drug lord, Nanjo Jones.

Goodbye Lonely (Book 4) - Kylie Bancroft was shy and had to resort to going to confidence classes. How could she win the love of Gareth Beecher, her faculty adviser, a man with a jealous ex-wife in his past and a current mystery surrounding a hand found in his garden?

Practice Run (Book 5) - Marcus Bancroft had many reasons to avoid Mount Faith but Deidra Durkheim was not one of them. Unfortunately, on one of his visits he was the victim of a deliberate hit and run.

Sense of Rumor (Book 6) - Arnella Bancroft was the wild, passionate Bancroft, the creative loner who didn't mind living dangerously; but when a terrible thing happened to her at her friend Tracy's party, it changed her. She found that courting rumors can be devastating and that only the truth could set her free.

A Younger Man (Book 7)- Pastor Vanley Bancroft loved Anita Parkinson despite their fifteen-year age gap, but Anita had a secret, one that she could not reveal to Vanley. To tell him would change his feelings toward her, or force him to give up the ministry that he loved so much.

Just To See Her (Book 8)- Jessica Bancroft had the opportunity to meet her fantasy guy Khaled, he was finally coming to Mount Faith but she had feelings for Clay Reid, a guy who had all the qualities she was looking for. Who would she choose and what about the weird fascination Khaled had for Clay?

The Three Rivers Series

Private Sins (Book 1)- Kelly, the first lady at Three Rivers Church was pregnant for the first elder of her church. Could she keep the secret from her husband and pretend that all was well?

Loving Mr. Wright (Book 2)- Erica saw one last opportunity to ditch her single life when Caleb Wright appeared in her town. He was perfect for her, but what was he hiding?

Unholy Matrimony (Book 3) - Phoebe had a problem, she was poor and unhappy. Her solution to marry a rich man was derailed along the way with her feelings for Charles Black, the poor guy next door.

If It Ain't Broke (Book 4)- Chris Donahue wanted a place in his child's life. Pinky Black just wanted his love. She also wanted him to forget his obsession with Kelly and love her. That shouldn't be so hard? Should it?

Contemporary Romance/Drama

After The End--Torn between two lovers. Colleen married her high school sweetheart, Isaiah, hoping that they would live happily ever after but life intruded and Isaiah disappeared at sea. She found work with the rich and handsome, Enrique Lopez, as a housekeeper and realized that she couldn't keep him at arms length...

Love Triangle: Three Sides To The Story- George, the husband, Marie, the wife and Karen-the mistress. They all get to tell their side of the story.

The Preacher And The Prostitute - Prostitution and the clergy don't mix. Tell that to ex-prostitute, Maribel, who finds herself in love with the Pastor at her church. Can an ex-prostitute and a pastor have a future together?

New Beginnings - Inner city girl Geneva was offered an opportunity of a lifetime when she found out that her 'real' father was a very wealthy man. Her decision to live up-town meant that she had to leave Froggie, her 'ghetto don,' behind. She also found herself battling with her stepmother and battling her emotions for Justin, a suave up-towner.

Full Circle- After graduating from university, Diana wanted to return to Jamaica to find her siblings. What she didn't foresee was that she would meet Robert Cassidy and that both their pasts would be intertwined, and that disturbing questions would pop up about their parentage, just when they were getting close.

Historical Fiction/Romance

The Empty Hammock- Workaholic, Ana Mendez, fell asleep in a hammock and woke up in the year 1494. It was the time of the Tainos, a time when life seemed simpler, but Ana knew that all of that was about to change.

The Pull Of Freedom- Even in bondage the people, freshly arrived from Africa, considered themselves free. Led by Nanny and Cudjoe the slaves escaped the Simmonds' plantation and went in different directions to forge their destiny in the new country called Jamaica.

Jamaican Comedy (Material contains Jamaican dialect)

Di Taxi Ride And Other Stories- Di Taxi Ride and Other Stories is a collection of twelve witty and fast paced short stories. Each story tells of a unique slice of Jamaican life.